# THE MAN IN THE CLOSET

# ROCH CARRIER

*translated from the French by*
*Sheila Fischman*

VIKING

VIKING
Published by the Penguin Group
Penguin Books Canada Ltd, 10 Alcorn Avenue, Toronto,
Ontario, Canada M4V 3B2
Penguin Books Ltd, 27 Wrights Lane, London W8 5TZ,
England
Viking Penguin, a division of Penguin Books USA Inc.,
375 Hudson Street, New York, New York 10014, U.S.A.
Penguin Books Australia Ltd, Ringwood, Victoria, Australia
Penguin Books (NZ) Ltd, 182-190 Wairau Road,
Auckland 10, New Zealand

Penguin Books Ltd, Registered Offices:
Harmondsworth, Middlesex, England

First published in English 1993

10 9 8 7 6 5 4 3 2 1

*Publisher's note: This book is a work of fiction. Names,
characters, places and incidents either are the product of
the author's imagination or are used fictitiously, and any
resemblance to actual persons living or dead, events, or
locale is entirely coincidental.*

Printed and bound in Canada on acid free paper ∞

**Canadian Cataloguing in Publication Data**

Carrier, Roch, 1937–
    [Homme dans le placard. English]
    The man in the closet

Translation of: L'homme dans le placard.

ISBN 0-670-84777-1

I. Title

PS8505.A77H613 1993    C843'.54    C92-095675-0
PQ3919.2.C37H613 1993

Other Roch Carrier
titles available from
Penguin Books Canada

Prayers of a Very Wise Child
Heartbreaks Along the Road

# CHAPTER 1

The sun is going down behind the pine trees. A broad lake of red ink drowns the pines, then languishes, soaked up by the black earth.

This is the moment when one is aware of the soul of life, the magical moment when light is transformed into night.

For Nicole and Pierre Martin, it marks the hour when the weekend is over. Now they must forsake the shelter of the hills, leave the country house, with its perfumes of idleness and good food and friendship. Every time, they experience the same little pang: they must abandon this place they love and journey to an unknown country. Their hesitation lasts only a moment. Once their car is on the road, the country weekend is already just an enticing memory.

The sky is clear and the setting sun is reflected in it as if in a beautiful grey mirror.

"The girls will have a fine week," says Pierre Martin.

"You can see that autumn's in the air," says Nicole, his wife. "It's the most beautiful time of year. Even if there were freezing rain, even if there were a snowstorm, the girls would have a fine week. I've never seen such joy as those girls possess. When I remember how I felt cornered at their age . . . bound by so many conventions . . . afraid of life . . . of everything. It's wonderful to see those girls enjoy their liberty and their appetite for life. And they're so beautiful . . . as beautiful as life . . . beautiful the way girls like me should have been when we were young."

"Nicole," Pierre confesses, "you make me want to go back to the house, where we left them!"

"Pierre Martin, you're showing your age when the thought of youth puts you in such a state . . . Let the girls have fun with other young people their age."

"I'm glad we lent them the house," says Pierre, his teasing smile gone now. "They'll enjoy it."

"Charlotte would trade all her exotic travels

for one week in the country in October. Whenever we lend her the house she says: Not even Istanbul or Bangkok or Prague is as beautiful as a little frost on the pine trees along the Gentle Rise Road!"

"And Johanne, the little actress, with that way she looks at things. Like a child in a theatre, fascinated by some marvellous show."

"Don't get too excited, old man!"

"All right, I know, I'm not allowed to touch. But can't I even look?"

Nicole sighs, looks at the cows gathered outside the stable.

"At my age, it's not easy to see your man always looking elsewhere . . ."

"You've got nothing to worry about, Mother!"

"I'm not your mother!"

"Can't we even tease any more? Teasing is a form of love."

Pierre hates these tense moments that always come after the warmth and peace of the weekends. He and Nicole are unable to take the harmony of the country home with them. They have to break it before they return to the city. Every weekend, when they're a few kilometres from their house, they have to live through this moment Pierre refers to as their "depression." They have to exchange some blows that aren't violent but that always wound a little. Afterwards, peace is restored and they go back to their routine.

As they do every Sunday night, they drive past the house of the Auberts. Good friends. The Auberts are famous in the village for the boat that's been under construction for years and has never left its scaffolding. For years now, the Auberts have been making preparations for a big trip. For years, with his own hands, Dr. Aubert has been polishing this boat until it gleams like a jewel. Stroking it seems to give him more pleasure than sailing it would. He is always postponing the decision to leave.

"Aubert and I," says Pierre Martin, "we're very different. He's building on the notion that he has to leave, while I build on the notion of stability, of permanence. Deep down, though, what fascinates him is stability, while with me it's what moves. I enjoy contradictions like that; they make life so fantastic and complex — and so interesting. While Aubert hasn't finished his boat, I've put up four towers."

"Some people prefer his boat to your towers . . ."

"I hope my towers don't float any better than his boat."

Pierre chuckles. They're not so unhappy after all.

"That boat's been there a long time," observes Nicole, as usual.

"How long can a boat keep itself from sailing?"

Now they're driving onto the highway access ramp.

"Aubert has his boat and his travels," sighs Nicole Martin, "you've got your towers standing at the street corners, and what do I have?"

"You have the children, you have me . . . and you have life . . ."

"Yes, life . . ."

And laden with weekend baggage, the car flies along the highway to where the city awaits the couple with a new week.

Pierre and Nicole assume that, as usual, they won't be back until the end of the week.

# CHAPTER 2

Before you let your wife and children into your home, check to see if a man is hiding in a closet. There is a rapist at large. We still know nothing about him — but we already know too much. He crept into a house as silently as the night. He said nothing, but his victim cried out.

This is the warning given to his readers by the journalist Barry Tremblay. His paper, *L'Écho du royaume du nord*, published here in the northern kingdom for the past fifty-three years, never stoops to bloody sensationalism, as do the big city papers. There must be a good reason for it to do so today.

This morning, all that remains of the matter is words. Repeated, poorly remembered, distorted words that merge into the chaos of memory and the shadows of the night. Words that try to make sense of events no one knows. Who can be sure that the events being talked about really occurred? And yet, there was blood.

People are afraid. A window was broken; glass splinters cut a young girl's hand. A car was spotted on the country gravel road.

This morning, heavy clouds sail above the secondary residences of the fancy folks from town, as the villagers call them. They are scattered through the spruce forest; they sit on hilltops or deep in the valleys. Isolated houses. From the road, they're invisible. The fancy folks from town come here to listen to the birds, to the wind in the branches. They come here to play with some noisy machine — they who all week have their souls locked inside their well-educated turtles' shells. They enjoy felling a tree or killing some animal, so they can share in the pleasure of ancestral memories. Has the poet of the North not said: "We are the grandsons of the sons of giants"? Aside from that, the country is deserted. Unless you live there, unless you have a secondary residence like the rich weekend people, you only end up there if you get lost.

Yesterday, in the middle of the night, in a house in the pines, an unknown man burst out of a closet. There were screams, a shattered window. Gravel was thrown up along the Gentle Rise Road by a car that was travelling too fast. Blood poured into the shattered window; it stained the white wall, too. That's what they say.

In this part of the North, all the houses have alarm systems hooked up to the telephone network. Gates with padlocks, doors with bars, security bolts protect them.

As for the rich people, they enjoy getting together up there: it's their idea of paradise. It's a community. Over dinner, washed down with several bottles of wine, they recount and they listen to the same stories as the Sunday before, which were the same as last year, as five years ago or ten. Suddenly there comes that moment of silence, like the one last week, like the one five or ten or even twenty years ago; and then someone pipes up: "Remember?"

For a long time they will say:

"Do you remember when Johanne, the actress, saw a man burst out of her closet?"

"I suppose she'd gone to bed naked?"

"A beautiful girl she was . . ."

"Yes, you thought so . . ."

"She was like a painting by Renoir."

"I prefer Renoir's curves to Picasso's cubes."

"Between that actress's curves and mine, you prefer . . ."

That's how they will talk, the people from town, when they're far from the tensions of the city, in their northern forest refuge, when they recall the events of the night of October 29.

Instead of clarifying the facts, words crumble into a haze of syllables. Of those events, there will remain only recollections of words, of accounts that cancel and contradict each other and then become transformed, their components tangled.

Did all that happen?

To keep from forgetting, perhaps a woman in the village cuts out the article from *L'Écho du royaume du nord* and pins it up by her telephone.

TERROR STALKS THE LAND! Our region's natural charms have drawn people who want to flee the sprawling towns, including many citizens who are well-educated and well-to-do. They make a major economic contribution to our northern kingdom.

We hope they will not succumb to terror, to say nothing of panic. When they come here to their secondary residences, will they worry about finding themselves face-to-face with a man in the closet?

Last night, a young unmarried woman staying in a house in the shadow of our beautiful forests lived through the nightmare of seeing a hefty man, whose intention was clearly assault, burst from a closet.

The woman, a lovely young actress with a fine future before her, was forced into having the fright of her life. She sprang from her bed, even though doing so exposed her anatomy, for the young woman was scantily clad for sleep. She hurled herself through the window after taking the trouble to break and shatter the glass.

She suffered cuts to the fingers, hand and arm but escaped her attacker, who vanished and is still at large. Be alert. Before you let your wife and children into your home, check to see if a man is hiding in a closet . . .

# CHAPTER 3

She sounds excited, nervous, breathless at the other end of the phone. Nicole Martin must certainly be pale. No one telephones so early in the morning. The city is asleep. It must still be totally dark.

With no apology for calling so early, she pours out all these words she can't hold back.

She says she's been awake since 1:36 a.m. At precisely that moment, the phone rang and woke her.

"It was like a shot. I thought Pierre was dead. He's had some mild heart attacks. I've always told him those attacks are tremors preparing the ground for the earthquake. Pierre wasn't home. He came in later. His car had skidded. The October rain had turned the road surface to ice. The car went out of control and into the ditch.

"Anyway, it wasn't Pierre on the phone. It was Charlotte . . . She was calling from the country. We'd lent her our house . . . She's there, yes, with Johanne, that's right, the actress. Johanne was terrified. Shaken up. In a state of shock. A fright. Couldn't speak. Charlotte told me everything. While the actress was asleep in her bed, a man came out of the closet."

"A strange man?"

"An actress doesn't keep her boyfriends in a closet."

On the telephone, Nicole is panting as if she's been running. Here, in her house in town, she maintains she can sense the man who burst out of that closet in the country. She feels as if he's in her own closet. Even though she's far from her northern countryside. She needs to talk so she can get over her fear. Pierre is still asleep.

"When Pierre came home shortly afterwards he was preoccupied. 'I could have been killed,' he said. He described the skid: the car spun around, the brakes useless, and he landed in the ditch. It happened on flat ground. There was no one around. And that cold from Trois-Rivières . . . Meanwhile, I don't know how, but a man got into our country house and hid in our bedroom closet. He waited for his victim and then he just materialized, like a ghost. The closet door creaks. Johanne was alone downstairs. She cried out for help. Charlotte couldn't hear her. She was asleep upstairs, with her head under the pillow. That's what she told me. So what happened? The man from the closet grabbed Johanne's face and clamped his hand over her mouth. Charlotte didn't hear anything because Johanne couldn't scream. After that, if I understood Charlotte correctly, Johanne managed to free herself. She broke a windowpane with her elbow and went outside, arms and hands bleeding, her body cut by the glass. She was naked. It was cold. . . . If the rain between Montreal and Trois-Rivières had turned to ice . . .

"How could a man get into our country house without breaking anything? without forcing anything? when there were two girls inside? How long had he been waiting inside the house? Was he there before the girls arrived? A man in the closet in my house: how will I ever go back there without thinking of him? How will I be able to live in my house when I know that a stranger can just walk in as if the door were wide open? Actually, he didn't break anything. He couldn't have had a key . . . Did the girls forget to lock the door? Young people scoff at precautions.

"Pierre is so absent-minded. Especially lately! His mind seems to be somewhere else. In the past, when the road was icy, Pierre always managed to keep his car under control. Why did he swerve last night? He must have been thinking about his tower downtown. He didn't even seem surprised when I told him Johanne had been attacked by a man who'd burst out of the closet. He barely reacted. He just said, 'I could have been killed,' then he told about skidding on that flat stretch, with no houses in sight, without even a point of light from a lighted window.

"'How did you get out of the ditch?'

"'I finally saw someone coming and I signalled. It was cold.'

"Not a single question about the man in the closet. He didn't even ask 'What happened to Johanne?' not even 'What did the man in the closet look like?'

"Pierre just went upstairs and went to bed. True, he'd had a fright too. He didn't say how deep the ditch was. From the look in his eyes, I'm sure it seemed deep to him. Poor Pierre! When he came in there was hay in his hair."

"Hay? That's strange."

"Grass . . . How can a man sneak into a house without being seen, without smashing anything, without battering anything down? A man's not a rat . . . Oh! just saying it gives me the shivers . . . A rat . . . Remember when I saw the rat, just sitting there on the Turkish carpet and staring at me? At first I thought my eyes were tired from reading and I wasn't seeing straight. But it was a rat all right. Heavens, I was frightened! As frightened as a woman can be in her lifetime! When I saw that rat I think I died for a few seconds. And then I came back to my senses and screamed. The rat didn't budge.

"And that was just a rat . . . not a strange man coming out of my bedroom closet in the dark when I'm naked in my bed . . . Johanne must have been scared to death. A natural, liberated woman like her sleeps without a stitch . . . Imagine, in the night, a man she'd never seen before: he touches her, she doesn't see him . . . Johanne's not the kind of girl to slam the door in a man's face, but I'm sure she wanted nothing to do with that one! Did he use a skeleton key to get in? He couldn't have, there's a burglar-proof lock. A Swiss security lock. The front door is like the door to a safe. The only person here in the country who has the key is Constant, our handyman. Though with his crutches he's more like a helpless-man! In the past he used to do favours for us. He can still keep an eye on the house, see that the doors haven't been forced, that the windows . . . The house is off the road and hidden in the pines. With those crutches, Constant can't be invisible or inaudible! The man in the closet slipped into the house like a ghost.

"I'll never feel comfortable in our country house again. I'll always be afraid of that vampire in the closet, waiting for night so he can attack a woman.

"We rarely let anyone use our country house. We're as selfish as the next one, but that's not why we keep the house for ourselves. It's important to know a house . . . A house is as fragile as a violin.

"Our house in the country is like a boat we can escape on . . . Charlotte knows it very well . . . If there's a plumbing problem it can be fixed, but what can be done about pretty Johanne's fear?"

# CHAPTER 4

At the very end of the night, along the horizon, something glitters and sparkles. It is the new-born day. Just as a nightmare passes, the man in the closet has gone away. The police chief has asked his stupid questions and gone home to sleep. Constant, the handyman, has left as well, after offering to sleep in his car and keep an eye on the place. He was uneasy. There was too much mystery in the house. He went from room to room in search of signs, of evidence. Finding nothing, he grew impatient. Finally he began to block up the shattered window. The nights are cold in October. And if there was a wind . . . He used big plastic bags and adhesive tape.

Johanne is shivering despite the layers of sweaters piled on over her dressing gown. The telephone has calmed down.

The nightmare hasn't gone away. It has just become invisible in the silence. People are still struggling to fathom what happened.

Last night, after a dinner of salad and fruit, Charlotte went to see a farmer's wife, to be measured for a skirt made of locally woven fabric. She'd met the dressmaker at the agricultural fair.

"I'll show you her weaving," Charlotte promised Johanne. "It's fantastic!"

She was gone a long time. When she came back she smelled of hay.

"It's the fresh country air," Charlotte explained. "It's so invigorating!"

"Did the dressmaker's husband want to show you his new cow?" Johanne quipped.

Charlotte didn't laugh.

"I'll tell you later," she promised, tossing a log on the fire. "This lovely stone fireplace is covered with soot," she added.

They opened their books. Without looking up, they began to talk. They laughed. Then they drank some beer. Then they smoked. They drank slowly. Smoked slowly. Johanne recalls that, for no reason, their voices were hushed, as if they were fearful of being overheard. Who could have heard the secrets of these two young twentieth-century girls?

Johanne shudders at the thought. Is it possible that even now the man is in the closet? At the end of the Gentle Rise Road, far from any neighbour, isolated as people were during the historic days of the colonization, can it be that even now they had a hunch that the man in the closet was listening to them? Johanne recalls very clearly that she heard a creaking sound. Does an old house creak that loudly in the autumn wind?

After much beer and many secrets, the young girls read to one another from the logs they kept of the stormy urban seas.

"If affection didn't exist in this life where so many are all alone . . ." said Charlotte.

Johanne thinks she remembers that for a long time they embraced and held one another, one girl's face nestling in the other's hair. It was good. It was the warmth of friendship. Standing in the middle of the living room . . . if Johanne had tried to walk she'd have fallen. She remembers that she kept saying, "My legs are like yoghurt!" and that she choked with laughter.

Finally, she got undressed in her room. She has no other memory of this part, but she shudders now at the thought of a stranger watching her. Those creaking sounds that should have worried her . . . "A modern woman learns how to deal with fear."

Her eyes were already shut. She was so sleepy. She was asleep before she even fell into her bed.

And the man jumped out of the closet: an earthquake. During the night, that shadow stole a few moments of her life.

Charlotte and Johanne thought they'd never get to sleep again because of the monsters hiding in the shadows, but their bodies can't bear the weight of the night any longer. Their eyelids are sealed. In thick voices, bidding each other farewell as if they were embarking on a long separation, the two young girls head for the bedrooms.

Charlotte disappeared into hers. At her door, Johanne stops for a moment, nauseated. This is ridiculous. The man has run away. He isn't in the closet now. What's left is his memory. Unshakable. She flicks the switch. She will sleep with the lights on. They're comforting. She is so tired. She can't see clearly. Is that a letter by her pillow? She doesn't remember seeing a letter in her bed. How odd, she thinks.

Perhaps the answer to all the questions, the explanation of what has happened, will be found in this letter. She is still afraid. She touches the envelope cautiously. Should she call Charlotte? No. Not right away. Later, she'll call her.

Why not now? Why refuse to share the secrets of her night of terror? Does she want to keep its mysteries to herself? Away from Charlotte's gaze, with trembling hands, Johanne starts to tear open the envelope.

As she is unfolding the letter, her stomach knots: she feels as if the man is there. Her body senses the disturbing waves of his presence. It seems that there's a hollow in her bed, as there was during the night, that now is as deep as a ravine. She is aware of his odour. A shudder zigzags down her back. There's no reason to be afraid: he's not there. She is alone. She can read. What a whirlwind last night's events have stirred up! The man in the closet didn't have a pungent smell like those who work with their hands. It was, rather, a delicate odour. Johanne is probably mistaken. What she thinks is a memory is only the perfume of the paper she holds in her fingers. Yesterday, she was a little drunk on beer. There was some magic smoke in her head.

The words had been put there by a computer.

Beloved,
I can't write *my* beloved, because you aren't yet mine, but perhaps you will be mine today. Never will there be such a glorious marriage of dream and reality, of my soul's desire and your

body's flesh. I hope my body will bring
happiness to your soul.

Johanne stops. It's hard to believe that these
words are actually written on the paper. She reads
it again. It all seems unreal. What is it about the
Martins' house that makes everything that exists
lose its solidity? How is it that the man in the
closet writes like a poet, then lies in wait for his
prey like a ravenous tiger?

People don't write this way nowadays. They don't love this way either. I
love in the manner of the gods and
goddesses who had so much love in
them, they could live on for centuries
after the blood had flowed from their
wounds. I love you as one loves at the
age of fifteen, when one wants to die
if the beloved rejects him. I love you
as, for years, I couldn't love you
because, beloved, you were not there.
I love you as one would love if one
could be at once fifteen years old and
a thousand.

Tonight, I will be able at last to
whisper how much I love you! Alas, my
lips are clumsy, barely able to give
bashful kisses.

And so I am writing this note. I must

shut away the wild torrents of my passion
inside these little letters. I want you to
know that every character is a spark of
my love, as vast and mighty as if all the
forests of Canada, Amazonia, Australia
and Scandinavia were set ablaze.

Several times, Johanne interrupts her reading.
Stunned, overwhelmed by the words, she loses
track of what she has read. Then she must start
again and reassemble the puzzle of these words.
Aside from the love it expresses, it could be a letter from a lawyer. That means the man in the closet
is no longer young: he didn't learn the language of
love from rock music. Why was she so frightened?
Why did she think she'd be strangled, raped, evis-
cerated by this man? Can a murderer preparing to
kill demonstrate so much naive tenderness?

The actress pulls herself up as if preparing to
attack:

"That's no way to think! You have to be pretty
dumb to be taken in by the prose of a rapist!"

Her sympathy for the writer of the letter, she
thinks, is quite simply the sympathy of the victim
for her executioner.

I'm only human but I am capable of
as much love as God, and who is God
but a person who loves more than all
others?

Charlotte is up. The morning smells of coffee.

"Charlotte," cries Johanne, "listen. 'I am capable of as much love as God . . . '"

"Are you learning your next part? That's from Claudel, or . . ."

"It's a declaration of love from the man in the closet."

"What did you say?"

"I found a letter from him in my bed."

"A letter?"

Charlotte rushes into the room.

"Show me."

As Johanne holds out the letter, Charlotte snatches it away. "Hand it over!" she says authoritatively. She drops it into her pocket.

"Maybe we should show it to the police?" Johanne suggests.

"You're a real actress!" says Charlotte impatiently. "You always need a director . . . That letter's mine. It was written for me. It was given to me."

"The assailant left it in my bed."

"Do you really think he intended to leave his card, like a detective?"

# CHAPTER 5

Around eleven o'clock, when the two friends go out to do some shopping, the villagers have already heard about the nocturnal goings-on. They want to know more. Charlotte has to repeat the story of their troubled night.

"It wasn't as hard on me as on Johanne . . . The poor thing didn't deserve such a fright! While I, I heard such a scream of terror, the blood froze in my veins. Johanne was so frightened, her screams were horrifying! Apparently the man who came out of the closet was turned on by smelling her nightgowns and slips. I didn't see him myself. Johanne never leaves home without

a complete wardrobe, in case she meets a guy.
Poor Johanne, how many guys do you know
who'll ask you to put your clothes on?"

The villagers ask the two strangers a question
that seems to be disturbing the soundness of their
judgment: why would two beautiful girls go and
stay by themselves in the forest, so far from the
road? What happened is not surprising . . . When
Little Red Riding Hood ventures into the woods,
she's bound to meet the wolf . . .

"It's not surprising that two lovely girls with
bodies like theirs would have attracted an animal
worse than a wolf: a man."

The joke was quoted and repeated. Everyone
in the village knew that the good smell of fresh
flesh, washed and perfumed, had been floating
around the house in the pines.

"Why did we come to the house? Because it's
beautiful," replies the actress. "The mountains
around it are something we don't have in the city.
And I'd rather see the mountains and the sky
outside my window than my neighbour's face at
his window, trying to see if I'm looking at him.
Here, we have the forest, fresh air. Here, you can
smell the autumn. You can feel the passing of
time. Time belongs to us; no one can steal it from
us. And that's why I came to your village."

In the grocery store, the villagers smile
incredulously. They aren't convinced that they
enjoy so many privileges. In their opinion, the

good life exists in town. It's colder here in these mountains than in other places, and the snow comes earlier.

"Instead of taking a holiday in the summer," Charlotte goes on, "I like to take a few days in the fall. It's the most glorious time of year. Autumn in Quebec — I wish there were no other season. A woman feels alive in the fall. The night and the day, stars and trees, the mountains and the river — everything's more beautiful in the fall. That's why I'm here. I know the Martins, who own the house. My father and Pierre Martin were students together in London. The Martins looked after me when I was little. They changed my diapers. It's perfectly normal for me to borrow their country house for a week. I think of all the affection they gave me when I was a child, and their friendship now."

What she says is true, of course, and the villagers know it. However, because of what happened, because of that man who burst out of a closet in the middle of the night, it's hard to believe anything now, even the simple things the two girls from town talk about. It seems that, because of that man, each of them is hiding a little something.

"I wanted to share the beauty of this area with my friend, Johanne. She didn't come here to have the fright of her life. I'm a lawyer and I specialize in divorces. Johanne's an actress. You may have seen her on television."

"There's so many people on the television . . . but your friend is certainly talented!"

What can a beautiful girl be looking for, so far from the city, at the end of a road that disappears into the trees? No one had an answer to that question.

"Johanne isn't lucky enough to have friends like the Martins. She doesn't take many holidays. Even when she isn't working, an actress is under pressure. In the acting profession, not working is as hard as working. Johanne is always worrying. She's a good friend and I wanted to share everything I have with her."

"Maybe one of you left the door open to attract a male," suggests an old pensioner with a pipe.

Everyone laughs at his joke, except of course the two girls.

"Actresses aren't like other people," Charlotte pleads. "They can easily forget a door, a window . . . Since we were alone in the middle of the forest, I took responsibility for checking the doors and windows, even the car doors and garage door, before it got dark."

"While you were closing the garage door, the man went and opened the door to the house. That's what happened!"

"The man couldn't have come in then. Johanne wouldn't have let him . . . She'd have called me . . ."

"She's an actress. They aren't like us," asserts a woman with a pointed chin who looks over her glasses and who is regional vice-president of the Association for the Protection of Life. "Everybody knows that actresses sleep around. When your friend saw the man, she probably liked his looks and pointed out the closet so he could hide there. An actress may cry out in the night, but not necessarily from fear . . ."

"Madame, if you dream about seeing a man come out of your bedroom closet," said Johanne, "I'm sure you'd rather it wasn't your husband!"

Much laughter. That actress certainly can be funny. The woman with the pointed chin takes off and the others draw closer.

"No way a man could sneak into that house," says Johanne confidently. "There's two possibilities: either he was there before us and he waited. But a man in a closet who doesn't move, doesn't eat, doesn't pee, is impossible. Or, the man had the key. He came in without making a sound. And there's one person with a key to the Martins' house. Constant. With his crutches . . ."

"There've been miracles before, and crutches that didn't stop anybody from running!"

"At his age, Constant wouldn't hide in a closet to scare a young girl . . ."

"Maybe it was just a bad dream?" Charlotte suggests. "Here in the forest, Johanne could have been overwhelmed by the silence, by the denseness of the night, the wind growling in the branches; perhaps some childhood fears came back and haunted her. Actresses are sensitive, very impressionable. It's their job. When they're happy, they're happier than other people. Sometimes, you know, a good actress can't distinguish between her imagination and reality . . . Johanne is a good actress . . . The sensitivity of actresses makes them react more intensely than ordinary people. That's what happened last night. Johanne believed that her nightmare was real. To escape it, she broke the window. I'm not saying she made everything up. I'm saying that, for her, the man in her nightmare was as real as a man who really did come out of her bedroom closet."

"It was no nightmare," the actress corrected her firmly. "Why do you keep insisting it was a bad dream?"

"Just in case no trace of the assailant is ever found."

# CHAPTER 6

A little later, the Martins come roaring into their paradise in the pines. They drove up as fast as they could, as soon as Pierre was awake, to assess the damages. The man in the closet has broken nothing, has left no marks on the carpet. He came and he left like the wind.

How did he get out of the bedroom? Did he jump out the window too? Did he pursue Johanne?

"Oh, I ran!" she says, and she sounds as if she's still out of breath. "I've never been so afraid. I've never been so afraid of a man. I could hear him breathing. In certain circumstances, men puff and blow like a bull. I could feel his breath on my neck. I was totally naked. I had no time to grab a nightgown or a sweater. I was barefoot and running through the woods. Normally, I can barely walk on a carpet without suffering, and there I was going barefoot through brushwood and weeds, over roots — and I didn't feel a thing. Not a thing . . .

"I heard the closet door creak. I heard the floor creak. Then I noticed a shadow moving among the shadows in my bedroom. I heard the shadow breathe. Then I saw it coming towards my bed. It didn't speak. It only breathed. When it tried to touch me, I screamed and screamed. I screamed as I've never been able to scream in our exercises at theatre school. I screamed as though my voice would help me escape. I'd forgotten that Charlotte was in her room."

"What makes you so sure it was a man?" asks Pierre Martin.

"Why would I be so frightened unless it was a man? I'm trying to describe how scared I was. I listen to myself and I can't begin to tell you how scared I was. I can't even remember how scared I was. Every drop of blood in my veins was replaced by terror, and then it left as if it had never been there . . . The man chased me. He tried to grab me by the neck. I could feel him clawing my shoulders."

"Let's have a look at your shoulders," says

Pierre Martin, "we'll see if there are any scratches. Show me."

"My husband went to bed late last night," Nicole Martin interjects.

Her tone insinuates that she hasn't said everything that's on her mind.

Johanne unbuttons her blouse and bares her shoulders, which are broad, round and muscular from swimming and ballet, then her arms . . .

"You're covered with scratches! Let's see a little more."

The actress undoes another button. With a horse-trader's eye, Pierre Martin studies the animal.

"That's a man's dream come true," says Nicole Martin. "Even my husband would be prepared to hide in a closet to get a look at a back like that. Johanne, you lovely child, the man who scratched you was no man. Pine needles scraped you when you were running away."

"That was no pine tree hiding in the closet!" Johanne protests. "All I remember is seeing the shape of a man. And I remember screaming. If I screamed that hard, it must have been because he threw himself at me. I can't remember. If he hadn't gotten on top of me I wouldn't have struggled so hard, wouldn't have screamed so loud. If he was in my bed, I must have the claws of a tigress. The man's back must be in shreds."

"Was your man short and thin, or short and

fat, or tall and skinny like my Pierre?"

The discomfort in Pierre Martin's eyes is so acute that Charlotte protests.

"Nicole, why are you dragging your husband into this?"

"He got home late last night, very late. My husband was very tired . . . He told me he'd skidded on an icy patch. He had a very rough night. He told me everything, except . . . He didn't mention the scratches on his back. I saw it, Pierre Martin, your back is torn to ribbons. Who did that to you?"

Pierre comes up to Nicole and lays his hands on her shoulders.

"My darling wife, we're old lovers, you and I, but when we let ourselves go, you're as passionate as ever, despite the years. My back always suffers when we make love . . . I love you the way you are, my beautiful Nicole."

Somewhat disconcerted by this unexpected declaration, Nicole Martin tosses her shoulders. Johanne laughs, and the four continue walking along a path through the coloured leaves of maples swirling in the wind.

"I really don't know anymore," says Johanne. "My mind is like a black hole. I ran for as long as I could. The man was behind me! Charlotte says she heard a car start. But now she's not sure. I didn't hear anything myself. Charlotte caught up with me. She found me because I was screaming.

I was screaming to drive away the fears that were mingled with the night. Then suddenly, when I saw Charlotte, I was like someone waking up. I saw that she hadn't taken the rifle. I reproached her. She said, 'I didn't want to risk hurting you.' That was a good reason. Charlotte's very wise. In those circumstances, being frightened like that, anyone else would have taken the rifle from over the bookcase and fired a shot at the shape that was moving through the pines. Charlotte thought, 'The shape that's moving there could be Johanne.'"

"Perhaps it was a nightmare, my poor Johanne. You don't shoot a rifle at a nightmare." Charlotte smiles.

# CHAPTER 7

Constant, the handyman, says:

"I sleep like a bear. A widower my age, he's got no worries. Not even death, though it'll be coming along. When the good Lord makes you as healthy as a horse, like He did me, death doesn't dare come too quick. My good health, it's better than a young man's, and it lets me work hard enough in the daytime that I'm tired when I go to bed. When I'm in my bed, I sleep. Now my late wife, when she was alive, many's the time she thought I'd passed away, I was that sound asleep. My wife died fifteen years and nearly two months ago now, in September, when school started . . .

No, I don't need pills for insomnia. When the phone rang last night, tell you the truth I didn't hear it. You get old, the eardrum thickens up."

"If you didn't hear the telephone, how do you know it rang?".

There is a tumble of laughter in the People's Savings Bank. Even the manager smiles: the scrawny little fellow with a face no wider than a knife-blade hasn't laughed more than once in his life, so they say. People still have fun trying to imagine what it was that set off such an exceptional reaction.

"The phone must have rung a few times," says Constant. "The girls in the Martins' house told me. It would've had to ring and ring before it shook up my old eardrums."

This morning, the elderly villagers received their monthly pension cheque from the government. There are six or seven of them at the People's Savings Bank, all of them upset at the story that's making the rounds, by telephone and word of mouth. An attack on a lovely young person from town: how could such a crime occur in their honest village? Such things happen in the cities, on television or in the newspapers.

"Life's different now . . ."

"If that's progress I prefer . . ."

"Would you tell me, Constant, how come those two beautiful girls phoned you? Surely there's somebody stronger than you in the village to defend them," declares a pensioner who's having a hard time holding onto his pipe, his tobacco, his match and his endorsed cheque.

"With them crutches, Constant, you can't even run," another pensioner suggests perfidiously, pointing his cane at the handyman.

Constant is used to defending himself in the village. He wasn't born here, wasn't brought up here. The others are wary of him, as they're wary of all strangers.

Constant came to the village when he was fourteen. God had given his father several sons, so he wasn't needed around the farm. As was the custom at the time, Constant left the family home. He went from door to door, offering his strong young arms. He was still just a child. No one needed a child. When night came, he asked permission to sleep in the hay, in a barn. He was exhausted. While he slept, a rat came and took from his bag the brown bread spread with maple sugar and cream that his mother had fixed for him. Constant didn't notice till morning. He was so hungry he felt a huge hole in his stomach, a burning. There weren't even crumbs left. Because he was just a child, Constant started to cry. The farmer found him in tears. They gave him a slice of bread with maple sugar. It wasn't as delicious as his mother's. Afterwards, they sent him out to pick blueberries, then to round up the herd.

From task to task, Constant spent three years with the farmer. He thought he'd found a family for the rest of his life. Unfortunately, one July day, while he was taking a nap in a haystack, the farmer died in his sleep. The widow remarried. Constant had to leave. He had become a man. He was strong. He'd learned how to work. He got back on the road, knocking on doors to offer his services. When they saw how tall and skinny he was, the farmers thought he'd be expensive to feed. Constant had saved a little money. He took a room in the village. It was in that village that he spent his life.

When Constant went back to the family that had adopted him, it was to fetch the young girl he would marry. She was the prettiest girl for miles around. "She was sunshine in a woman's dress," to quote Norbert, who had wanted her but hadn't won her. Norbert would never forgive Constant for stealing her away.

No one in the village would forgive Constant. A stranger from the next village, who had found a haven in this village where everyone had gone to the same school and the same church, Constant had taken something that didn't belong to him.

When Constant's wife died, everyone but Norbert came to the funeral. There were those who thought (and some actually said it out loud): "That woman could have lived a hundred years if she hadn't had to put up with a stranger." Without another word, but with the air of knowing much more, people looked off in the direction of the parish whence Constant had come. You could see its church steeple on the hill.

Only the fancy folks from town trusted Constant. He became the handyman for the well-to-do who bought up hectares of the hillside. They didn't know how to drive a nail or start up a pump when the water froze. Thanks to their incompetence, Constant discovered himself to be a carpenter, mechanic, gardener, meteorologist, tree grower. He even knew about healing with plants, if necessary. Basically, he knows whatever the city folks think he knows.

"If you ask me, Constant, it was you that was hidden in that closet," says a man who is counting the money the teller handed him. "You didn't hear the phone because you weren't at home, you were there with the girls . . . You're a man that's been without a woman for a long time. Everybody knows you've got a greedy nature. It's no secret."

Constant defends himself.

"At my age, my nature doesn't keep me awake nights. I'm a sound sleeper."

"Nature goes to sleep alright, but it wakes up in the spring. A man's still a man . . ."

"After the phone rang in the middle of the night, I pulled on my pants and jumped in the car and went over there: two little girls were being threatened. It was dark, gentlemen, dark like it gets in October. And in that darkness was a man who didn't want to be seen. My idea was to surprise him. I drove there with my lights off."

"Just like I said, you didn't want to be seen!" the man concluded, stuffing his money into his deep pocket and leaving the bank, smiling like a man who has been guaranteed a long life.

# CHAPTER 8

At 1:18 a.m. on the night of October 29, the telephone rang. My wife answered and I went back to sleep. We have a peaceful village here, with a sound administration and a good mayor. In my position as chief of the municipal police force and sole policeman, I'm not wakened every night by the call of duty. In fact, in the case of wrong-doing people tend to wait until morning to call me. Whenever I'm wakened at night in line with my responsibility for justice, it's generally on account of some stranger. Our own gallant citizens spend their nights sleeping and their days working.

"I didn't sleep long. My wife shook me and I looked at my watch: 1:19. I got out of my bed faster than a fireman. It was my duty. I'm also the chief of the volunteer firemen.

"Georgianna said to me:

" 'Wake up, Aurélien, you have to go over to the Martins' house. There's a man in the closet.'

"Georgianna didn't have to say it twice. I said to her:

" 'What's a man doing in the closet in the middle of the night?'

" 'Scaring the two girls that are staying in the Martins' house, you know, the one with the red chimney, hidden away in the pines beside the Gentle Rise Road.'

" 'Those girls have seen plenty of men up close. Why were they scared?'

" 'Because a man hidden in a closet makes more of an impression than a man in a bed,' said Georgianna.

"I'm reporting what she said because a well-written report contains all the facts. I don't believe those two young female persons run very far when a man comes near them. I've spotted those two lovely girls before, when I was out on my municipal surveillance rounds. I knew right away where they were staying. I'd noticed one of them a few times before, with the Martins. Monsieur Martin looked pretty pleased with himself because he was walking beside a beauty imported from town. The other one's an actress, from what they tell me, because I gathered all the information. She's an actress I don't remember seeing on TV. She can't be a great actress. They were alone in the Martins' house.

"During the week, the city folks have to work in town because that's where their jobs are.

"As chief of the municipal police, I have a duty to keep my eyes open. I went to the Gentle Rise Road several times and I slowed down in front of the Martins' house because I was thinking to myself, good thing our population's well-behaved. Two lovely strangers from town with long hair and grapefruits like they don't grow them around here, that's appealing.

"Faster than my Georgianna can write, I made my way to the Martins' house. According to the clock on my dashboard it was exactly 1:21 a.m., but that clock's always slow.

"The night was as black as dark-blue ink and I formulated this thought: If the girls that were staying at the Martins' could see a man in a closet, somebody must've turned on a light. Who? The man? The girls? When you've got experience, it refines your reasoning powers.

"During the interrogation, the girl that saw the man in the closet — the actress — advised me as follows: she couldn't turn on the light because she was paralyzed with fright; she jumped through the window; her fear made her feel strong enough to break down the wall.

"I saw nobody near the Martins' house. In the pitch-black night, someone could have been hiding under the trees. I shone my flashlight around but nothing stirred: not a man, not a woman, not a deer. Everything was quiet. I didn't spot any cars, either.

"During the surveillance tours I'm obliged by duty to make every day, I'd noticed nothing peculiar in the vicinity of the Martin house. The two girls seemed very quiet when they took a walk to breathe in our fresh country air. At night, I saw no abnormal lights around the house. It's true the pines are numerous and close together. No abnormal music reached my ear that might have warned me if anyone was enjoying themselves a little too much. A couple of times, I've noticed Constant's car on the Gentle Rise Road. Our old national tomcat's always called on whenever the folks from town don't know how to use a screwdriver. That old coot isn't the kind who'd refuse to fix a tap for two beautiful girls that are round where it's good to be round. Aside from that, I didn't notice anything special.

"On the night of the incidents in question, like they say in court, I found no signs of a car. At this time of the year, the ground is frozen. I ran my flashlight carefully over the gravel and I can't report any evidence of a car driving away in a cloud of dust. If the man from the closet took off by car, he went as quietly as an honest man whose conscience is clear.

"When I got to the Martin house that night I knocked at the door. I knocked several times. Fairly hard. There was no answer. I yelled: 'Police!' and then somebody turned the key in the lock. As I was walking in I thought, if you want to get in here, either you need an invitation or you need the key. I asked the girls: 'Before the incident, were you alone? Or was there a person with you of the same sex as the man in the closet?' Both of them answered, together and separately: 'We were alone.' Then I asked: 'Do you suspect anybody, preferably a man, that could have got in here after you were in bed?' They both assured me: 'No!' So then I said: 'Show me the bed by the closet.'

"I proceeded to examine the scene of the crime. The two girls were sleeping on different floors of the house, hence in different bedrooms. The closet is an ordinary closet with a door and lots of women's clothes. Not much room for a man unless he was skinny.

"The main facts that I observed, because they were visible, are as follows: Everything was normal in the Martin house. There were no battered doors, no broken locks. No ladder, no rope a person could have used to come down the chimney. With the aim of infiltrating into the house, that man from the closet didn't need to break a thing. The alleged victims, under the shock of the assault, assured me they had no visitors, either male or female or any other sex.

"On the quilt of the alleged victim's bed I observed the following objects: an open book with a difficult title, a letter, and two or three magazines with pictures of brassières and perfume bottles. I did not inspect the alleged victim's bed. No rape occurred and a happily married man has got no business sticking his nose into an actress's bed.

"I saw no signs of a struggle. No rugs had been shifted, no furniture overturned, no vases or statues broken. No blood, except on the glass fragments that were still attached to the inside frame of the bashed-in window. The projectile, probably a human body, had been propelled from the inside, because I picked up shards of glass on the balcony outside. I also counted eight drops of blood on the white paint of the wall of the house that was painted white. The actress confirmed that she'd bashed in the window with her own arm and shoulder.

"A number of empty bottles counted in the garbage testify that those girls drank a lot of beer, either during the week or yesterday.

"In the closet I found no fingerprints, no wire, no hairs, no clothing, no cigarette ashes.

"The most obvious fact to note was the fear of the two young girls. The actress was trying to talk but she kept running out of breath, as if she'd run to the village and back. Charlotte, the one that didn't see the man, not in the closet or anywhere else, remained silent as if she didn't dare to say a word.

"I smelled the smell of smoke in the house — a kind of plant I've smelled before in other circumstances because the young people nowadays smoke all kinds of plants. All the butts in the ashtrays had red on them, probably from the smokers' lips. I was unable to identify any male cigarettes. I deduce that the man from the closet was a non-smoker. And here's another observation. Charlotte, who didn't see the man from the closet, was behaving like the mother of a frightened child. She had her arm around Johanne's shoulder.

"I wouldn't want to leave out one last detail. It's been reported by I don't know who that yesterday, the Martins' blue car was seen on the Gentle Rise Road. That information must be verified. It would be an unusual occurrence. The Martins always arrive at their house around 10:15 on Sunday morning.

"This is my report as written by me but put down as usual by the expert hand of my wife Georgianna, who is my right arm even though she writes with her left.

"Aurélien Bouleau
"Chief of Municipal Police"

# CHAPTER 9

Early that morning, Nicole Martin told Madame Aubert about the man in the closet. She also described how her husband, Pierre, had skidded on the highway.

"Fortunately the car didn't overturn — he'd never have got out alive . . . What a night of emotions and turmoil!"

"While I," laments Madame Aubert, "I was fast asleep as if nothing had happened."

Immediately she phoned her husband's office. Just then, Dr. Aubert was listening to a patient lying on the couch in his office. He returned his wife's call later.

"It's urgent!" Madame Aubert had proclaimed. She told the doctor all the details. He listened, saying frequently, "Uhuh . . . Uhuh . . ." At the end, he announced: "I'm cancelling all my appointments."

Everyone knows his blue house. It has yellow shutters decorated with crescent-moon cut-outs. Dr. Aubert shakes your hand five times a day. He always forgets that he's seen you before. Whenever he sees you, he is meeting you for the first time.

No one understands exactly what he does. He's a doctor, but not really a doctor because, as they say, "He doesn't try to cure your diseases!" There are those who think he's a Protestant minister.

In the car, Dr. Aubert listens as his wife repeats for the fourth time, the fifth, what Nicole Martin told her on the telephone. Dr. Aubert nods and punctuates his understanding with "Uhuh . . . Uhuh . . . Uhuh . . ." His wife's account is as precise as though she had witnessed the events herself.

Finally they pull up in front of their house. Dr. Aubert concludes: "A good many abnormal things seem to have occurred." Rifle in hand, striding aggressively, he heads for the door of their house. If anyone is hiding in a closet, he won't hesitate to paste the mouth of his rifle against that person's chest, beside the heart.

The villagers have given the Aubert house a name: "the house with the boat." For years they've watched the doctor assemble the skeleton of a boat, put the finishing touches on the framework, watched him weave the shell. For a long time now, a beautiful white boat has been floating on stilts that are planted in the earth.

Ever since he was a child, Dr. Aubert has dreamed of sailing around the planet.

He dreams of sailing as others dream of having wings. For years he has sawn, cut, planed, sanded, hammered. The boat is ready to sail across the seas of the world, but the only water that has touched it is the rain. When it comes time to set sail, Dr. Aubert always finds this to finish, that to polish, this to replace, that to adjust, this to correct. And: "The suppliers are slow." To sail his boat around the planet: he toys with that dream every day. He reads books about the sea, takes courses in navigation. For hours at a time, holding compass and callipers, he navigates on his maps.

He dreams of sailing, yes, but as he was building his sailboat he discovered how much he enjoys construction, too. Handling wood is as good as floating on the sea; sawing is as pleasant as sailing close to the wind; planing as satisfying as luffing.

Dr. Aubert pushes open the door as if he were bashing it in. The noise, the shock show his determination to the man in the closet, if there is one. Ready to fire, to kill, to make a hole in a living chest, Dr. Aubert goes from bedroom to bedroom, closet to closet, room to room, from the basement to the attic. The house is empty. It does not shelter the monster he would have liked to destroy. Windows, doors — nothing has been forced. His precious wine cellar has not been violated. In the peaceful darkness only a spider has spun a web, which he unravels with the tip of his barrel.

Later, as he carves a roast of beef, rare, the way he's always liked it, Dr. Aubert explains the mysteries of the human soul. His wife listens, uttering "Uhuh . . . Uhuh . . ." in agreement, as she has learned to do from him.

"One must make the distinction," he argues, "between the real and the imaginary. The Martins' window was broken by one of the two girls when she ran away. An intruder can't sneak into a house without breaking something. When no material damage has occurred, the intruder can only be imaginary. Consequently, the man in the closet was imaginary. He didn't emerge from the night or the forest but from the mind of the young girl, who, as well as being a young girl, with all the passions and desires of her age, works in the acting profession. And what does that strange profession consist of? Of maintaining, and encouraging others to maintain, that reality is not what it is.

"As Heim showed so well, our wishes are linked to our weaknesses. Dreaming is often a way to compensate for that which we do not have or do not dare. Again, as Heim shows so clearly, by dreaming we show that we are at least capable of having wishes and of fulfilling them, in our sleep at any rate. In the case of the young actress, the possibilities are twofold. Either she wished deep down that there was someone in her bedroom. Was it a desire to be violated? I don't know. To know that, one would have to listen to her. Did she want to be violated by her father, by a thug dressed in leather, by a bishop whose ring she had just kissed? I don't know. I would have to know how the man in the closet was dressed. That detail hasn't been mentioned. Nothing is innocent; that failure to mention apparel in her dream is quite significant. By definition, the young actress enjoys theatrical effects. She had hoped, in her romantic fashion, that she would be seduced like someone in a play, *Romeo and Juliet*, say, or *Cyrano de Bergerac*. Let me draw your attention to the fact that, just as in both these plays, the young actress's bedroom opens onto a balcony. Or . . ."

"How do you know her room opens onto a balcony?" snaps his wife.

"In the world of the imagination, which is merely another vantage point for experiencing reality, everything behaves as it should. Another explanation is possible: namely that the man who emerged from the closet was the young actress herself. She was so frightened that she hurled herself through a window. In reality, what she feared was her own yearning to be violated. An impossible violation, of course. This young actress has sensed the birth of a beast within herself. It was that savage, masterful beast who appeared last night on the interior stage that is the soul of the individual.

"More likely, a young actress who sees a man burst out of her bedroom closet in the dark is, objectively, merely witnessing the depiction of her own desire. This young person undoubtedly dreamed about a man. She gave herself to him. It was only a dream. Only a dream can enter a house without breaking anything. There you are . . . Finish off the Julienas if you want, I'm going out to look at my boat."

The boat is famous. On Sunday, people drive along the Gentle Rise Road and slow down for a look at the doctor's boat, as they call it. Dr. Aubert likes to walk around it, gaze at it, stroke its keel the way you stroke a horse's breast.

"You know," Dr. Aubert goes on, "a dream like that is very significant, as are most dreams. In her autobiography, Agatha Christie describes how, as a small child, she was pursued by the nightmare of a man threatening her with a revolver . . . That dream is very eloquent to anyone who can decipher it . . . All her life, Agatha Christie tried to free herself of that nightmare by bringing it under her control: all her life she wrote stories about murder. What will become of the young actress's nightmare in the future? Everything is in the realm of the imagination, that is the site of the only reality."

Dr. Aubert dons the old red jacket he likes to wear in the country. It's a relief from the tight necktie and narrow suit jacket he must wear in his clinic. The day is cold. The air is dry. He lights a cigar. The countryside smells so clean, everything smells so new. It seems as if everything is beginning. Yes, one day he'll go away on his boat, but why go now? Life is so good here. And the sailboat isn't ready . . . But where is it? Where is his sailboat? It's not there! Is it on the other side? Did he look carefully? The stilts aren't supporting anything!

"Simone! Simone!" cries Dr. Aubert. "Simone! Someone's stolen my boat! My boat! Simone!"

His heart is pounding. His eyes fill with tears. He rushes towards his wife. He would like her to embrace him like his mother.

"Maybe you're dreaming," she says.

# CHAPTER 10

Charlotte is genuinely upset by what happened. She wishes it didn't show, but I'm a woman and I know how to look, I can see without seeming to be looking. Just from the way she said, "Oh, Nicole, it's you; you've come too," I realized something had really touched Charlotte.

Of course Pierre didn't notice anything. Men only notice what they want to. The third button of Charlotte's blouse was undone and you could see her lilac brassiere. This view of Charlotte's anatomy didn't escape Pierre. He told me:

"I'm an architect, after all. Do you get jealous when I admire the lines of a Gothic cathedral?"

Pierre avoids serious conversations. He runs away. For some time now he's been running away from whatever I'm concerned about . . . I can't tell him what I'm thinking any more. He won't communicate. Whenever I say anything he thinks I'm exaggerating.

"What am I supposed to look at?" he says. "Would you rather I looked at her feet? I felt uncomfortable seeing Charlotte again. I didn't know how to look at a woman who's so upset because of a man. You're right, Charlotte was badly shaken. I sensed she was a little ill at ease when she saw me. I'm a man. She probably can't make the distinction between the man who frightened her half to death and one who's as unthreatening as I am."

"A man's a man!"

Perhaps I spoke too abruptly. I can't talk to Pierre the way I used to; he doesn't listen the way he used to.

One thing's certain, I'm going to insist that Pierre let me see his back. I'll tear off his shirt if I have to. When Pierre went to take his shower this morning I saw marks on his back. I didn't pay any attention, but when I saw Johanne's shoulders all marked by the pine branches, I suddenly saw what I hadn't really seen this morning: Pierre has fingernail marks on his back. I'll check them out . . . It's probably nothing.

I know I want to have seen scratches on

Pierre's back. They're probably marks from the creases in the sheets. If I didn't react when I saw Pierre's back this morning it's probably because it wasn't important. If there'd been a reason to react, I'd have reacted. I'm not happy now the way I used to be. So I have a tendency to imagine problems. I ought to be happy: Pierre certainly has flaws like any man, but he's a good man, a big boy really, who's getting older too. Like all men as they get older, he's become fascinated with youth. They imagine someone else's youth can erase the passage of time in their own lives.

Is it age that's given me less aptitude for happiness? With time, our muscles stiffen. The heart is a muscle too. They say it's the seat of happiness.

It's not Pierre's fault that time is passing too quickly and turning me into an old woman. I mustn't reproach him. Men don't realize that time works on them, too. That's why they don't understand women. Pierre should pay a little more attention to me, he shouldn't let me drift alone on my raft while he looks on from the shore, as if to say that nothing has happened. I'll feel better once I've seen his back!

As for Charlotte, she's the essence of youth. How wonderful it was to watch that little girl grow up! She was made for life just the way it is. I know her as well as if she were our own daughter. She never went through those adolescent crises when you feel that you're too small for life, and think life is too small for your dreams. Charlotte has never been foolish. Charlotte is life with a smile. Charlotte is life with no self-doubts. Charlotte knows that life could be made differently but she's convinced that it's better to take what is than to dream about what is not. Charlotte always seems to be biting into a juicy apple. For her, the whole world is a delicious fruit. She threw herself into travelling to the other end of the earth with such curiosity, such hunger! She's seen misery, too. Poverty, slavery seen by Charlotte become something else. She always finds something beautiful in misery, something good. What an appetite she has! And then her work, being a lawyer . . . She bit into that, as well! She'd barely finished law school when already she had cases to plead. Charlotte doesn't bite like a tigress or a shark as some lawyers do; she bites like a beautiful girl biting into a fine, ripe fruit. Charlotte reminds me of an apple: round, tasty, juicy, fragrant, fresh. I'm not surprised that Pierre looks at her. He must want to touch her, too. Charlotte has never turned down a man. Oh yes, she's shaken a lot of branches in the orchards of men . . . I love Charlotte — and I'm jealous of her! She's a girl who takes everything while seeming always to give.

I can understand how a girl who's so good would be shaken by an idiotic pervert who hides in a closet to attack a woman. When you know that life is so beautiful, it must be disconcerting to meet such a pathetic monster. Charlotte will live. And in time, she'll discover other monsters . . .

As for you, Pierre Martin, it would be best if you don't have any fingernail marks on your back!

# CHAPTER 11

As my grandmother would have put it, thinks the librarian, I was talking through my hat. I may have ruined a man's life. Now what will happen to him? I didn't mean to do him any harm. The police chief came to question me. Had I really recognized Monsieur Martin's blue car? I can't swear to it. Hundreds of cars like it are driving around the province. No, I didn't note the licence number. I don't even know my own. I hate numbers. I see too many during the day. No, I didn't notice anything peculiar about it: no dents, nothing hanging from the rear-view mirror. Originally I assumed it was the Martins' car, but I was intrigued: they never come to their house before noon on Saturday. At first I said I'd seen the Martins' car, but then I had doubts. Was it really their car?

Running them over in my mind, I remember quite clearly, in logical sequence, the events that occurred yesterday, Monday, the day the man emerged from the closet.

It was around seven p.m. Usually it's very dark at that hour, but the western sky still bore traces of light. The road was silvery. The conifers looked more blue than green, while the other trees were already bare of leaves. With their naked trunks and branches they looked like skeletons. What I find most beautiful is the air. You can't see the air but you can say "It's beautiful," because it smells so good! No wine in the world, not even the wine that was buried with the kings of Mesopotamia, tastes as fine as our country air early on a late-October evening. No woman in the world, not even Queen Cleopatra who bathed in the milk of young goats and who had her body anointed with sweet oils mixed with powdered gold, no one has skin as soft as the evening air.

And that's the air I breathe when I go jogging. What joy! When I jog I'm conscious of the act of breathing. Most people will stop breathing one day without ever being aware that before they died, they breathed. Jogging has also made me aware of the beating of my heart. People look for happiness in all kinds of projects and ventures. Those earthbound grouches are anxious, sad that they aren't happier. They never stop to enjoy the greatest happiness available to a human being: to feel your heart beating!

Jogging gave me back my freedom of movement. Now I'm not a prisoner of my library or of the choir-loft in church where I play the organ. I'm someone who likes change. Every day I change my route. Yesterday was Monday. Monday: that's the day I take the Gentle Rise Road.

So, as I do every Monday, I headed west along the main street in the direction of the church; when I got to the bank I turned left, towards the church. I ran around the cemetery. It's the prettiest spot in town, like a lovely garden full of flowers. Too bad there are dead people in it. I think the old grey wood grave-markers are even more beautiful than the flowers. They give off a perfume of eternity. Everything smells good in a graveyard. Is it the souls of the dead that have per-fumed the air? I'd love to jog in the cemetery, along all those lovely paths that run through the green grass. It would be disrespectful to run where everybody is condemned not to move.

After that I took the Twisted Road, which begins at the wild raspberries. They've grown up in the place where, in Mama's day, her father's blacksmith shop used to stand, the one that burned down the day the Second World War broke out.

I like the Twisted Road because of the hills: you can't see what's on the other side. Overhead you always have the beautiful blue sky with clouds sailing in the October wind. I like the curves, too, which offer as many surprises as the hills. When I run it seems as if it's the landscape that's moving, that's waltzing in front of me. Because of the valleys and the hills, you think the forest is moving like the sea. With the rhythm of running it seems as if the road is moving, too, beneath my feet. You gaze at the sky starting to fill with stars and you feel Earth turning under your feet. Cottages are scattered here and there. They are modest; they hide themselves.

Then the Twisted Road crosses the Gentle Rise Road, which leads directly to Twenty-Nine Road: apparently there was a farmer who once had twenty-nine children. I must check that historical detail in the parish archives.

The Gentle Rise isn't all that gentle; naturally, I ran past the Martin house, which is surrounded by harmoniously planted pines. Nothing special. A breeze came up: it was as if it were pushing the greyish, smokey light through the branches. Some mist was floating, too. That's where I noticed the little white rump of a deer leaping across the stream.

As I do every Monday, I went as far as the old barn that's virtually abandoned. No symphony is as beautiful as the nocturnal music of Earth when animals and insects bid one another goodnight before they go to sleep.

Beside the barn, I noticed Monsieur Martin's blue car. I thought, it can't be here, it's not the weekend. Because of my musical training, my ears are quite sensitive. From the stable I could hear hay being crumpled, like paper. I thought, the cold weather is coming and the little animals are preparing their winter shelter.

When I got closer, I thought I heard someone moaning or weeping, or the shriek of a female cat, or the amorous lament of a porcupine. And I thought: It isn't the mating season.

This morning when I got to school, the teachers were talking about the latest news. I have no interest in that idle morning chatter when everyone sounds like a stutterer, repeating the same story. I wasn't really listening, but I heard someone announce, as if the news was worthy of the front page of *Le Figaro* in Paris: "A man was seen in the Martins' house!" I said, "That's not so amazing, I saw Monsieur Martin's car."

At that moment, I didn't know that a male monster with a carnivorous appetite had hidden in the closet to wait for night and throw himself at a buxom young actress. The assailant can't be Monsieur Martin. He's such a distinguished man.

Someone repeated that I'd seen his car. The police knew about it. I'd be the last one to believe they could accuse him.

There are thousands of cars just like Monsieur Martin's on the market. Monsieur Martin isn't the kind of man to hide in a closet. He's too well educated. He's a man who likes books. "Tell me you like books and I'll tell you that you respect people." I learned that proverb from a colleague of mine, a librarian from Ghana.

# CHAPTER 12

Only one thing matters in life, the apprentice journalist Barry Tremblay tells himself: the truth. As I look at my own face in the mirror today, I acknowledge the following truth: I want out of this godforsaken hole. The man in the closet will help me. Before anyone else, I shall unmask him. As a matter of fact, was he masked? He had the night to hide his face. What raw material for my first novel! I could call it *The Man Masked by Night*. No, too poetic, I'll try to find something as dry as a brand name: *Rape* or *Closet*, or perhaps something suggestive: *No Time for Pajamas*! Or why not *Naked Through the Window*?

Don't get carried away, Barry Tremblay! Your imagination is a fiery steed. Very well. It also has to be fed. Even if it's pathetic, journalism is a better provider than literature. So, let's draw up a three-point plan of attack: 1) I gather information and verify it; 2) I analyze my information and define its meaning, discrepancies and points of convergence; 3) I draw my conclusion and the guilty man is uncovered. Fantastic!

If I unmask the frustrated man who hid in a closet to seduce a young actress, they won't be able to refuse me a job on a real newspaper whose readers will read something else besides the article that lists the price of peas.

First certainty: A man who attacks a young girl like that, in the dark, is necessarily an individual who is unfulfilled. His behaviour established the fact that he's a person with a weak vocabulary: his language is assault rather than rhetoric. (If my own writing style is anything like my thought processes, I'll never get a job on a real newspaper.)

One point troubles me. The assailant didn't leave a single trace. Which is impossible. In criminal matters, there's no such thing as anonymity. The criminal always signs his work. If the criminal doesn't leave traces or fingerprints, then he leaves a visiting card, a note. Our rural Jack the Ripper took to his heels without leaving anything behind.

We cannot rule out any possibility. The two girls are in agreement: that's suspicious to begin with. Everything about this business is fishy. Nothing is particularly clear. That's suspicious. Let's investigate. And may intuition and reason cooperate and complement each other!

I don't rule out the possibility that the municipal police chief may be the man in the closet. I've checked on his comings and goings. What was he doing on the night of the events in question? According to his wife, he was in bed. Before I came along, our newspaper's Maigret, Valère Labranche, had covered crime in the region for forty-seven years. At his retirement party he warned me: "Never believe the testimony of a woman who hates her husband, or that of a woman who loves him."

Pierre Martin's blue car was seen here. Why would he come during the week? For years now, he and his wife have just been coming for the weekend. The proof that he didn't come and wasn't supposed to come: he and his wife had lent their house to two young girls. Let's mull over everything. Leave no stone unturned. Male instinct being what it is, even the educated man, whose savage instincts have been most watered down by his intelligence, is still a hunter. Given the quality of the does behind the tranquil pines along the Gentle Rise Road, it's possible that any man could lurk in a closet and wait for the appearance of a beautiful creature — even the great architect Pierre Martin.

I don't like the notion that I could have been the man in the closet. Unfortunately, I have to acknowledge that I possess practically all the qualities needed to play that role. Why not come right out with it: I'm frustrated. I can't wait to get out of this hole.

It takes less strength to pounce on a woman at night than it takes to convince her in broad daylight that you're the only man on the planet. I'm as lazy as any man who looks for the easy way out. There's nothing to prove I'm not the man in the closet. I'm the only one who knows, so I mustn't forget that the man in the closet is just like me if I were that man: straightforward, hypocritical, lazy, cowardly, fearful, so ordinary that no one suspects him. That man was an average man, a mediocre hunter.

Another assumption: the man in the closet was a perverse actor who knows tragedy like the back of his hand. He forced the actress to play the part of a victim, a role she'll never forget. Whenever she opens her eyes in the night, she will see the black shape of a man moving towards her. No curtain will erase him. Never again will the dark hold silence for her.

Enough philosophy, Barry Tremblay! What we need is a resolution to this affair! Get moving! Let's proceed methodically. First of all, I am not the man in the closet because I know he's not me! I'd have a hard time proving it's not me.

Last night, a prisoner escaped from the regional prison. Some people have suggested the escapee could be the man in the closet. Bad intentions are always attributed to those poor devils. The mathematical probability of the escaped prisoner's ending up in our village is very slight. Anyway, why would a prisoner break out of a cell just to hide in a closet?

Some people hint that the assailant was invited by the two girls. That hypothesis would explain why neither doors nor windows were forced. It cannot be supported. The two girls wouldn't have succumbed to terror if they'd known the assailant's face. Besides, if someone known to them had suddenly behaved aggressively, two strong, independent young girls would have been able to make him regret his unwise behaviour.

A nightmare can pass through walls and cause no damage; that's Dr. Aubert's theory. The actress maintains she saw a flesh-and-blood man bending over her. It's not impossible that she is refusing to admit she had a nightmare. We can't rule out that possibility.

The key . . . The man in the closet had the key. Who has access to a key to the house on Gentle Rise Road? The owners themselves. Nicole Martin is not implicated. Pierre Martin? His car was seen on the night of the attack. He himself was not seen. Perhaps it was a car that looked like his? Pierre Martin doesn't despise young girls in the bloom of youth. He has a way of looking at a skirt. It's always possible to err in judging someone, but he doesn't seem like a man who would attack a guest in his own house.

If Pierre Martin had wanted to seduce the young actress, he'd have arrived with flowers, books, champagne. No one would have been frightened.

I cannot justify feeling any suspicion towards him. I'm not forgetting that he's a man; two lovely, unattached girls are staying in his house and he has at least one key. Let's not rule out Pierre Martin, even if no suspicion hangs over him. Pierre Martin as the man in the closet: that's rather interesting.

Who else could have used the key? Constant. As handy-slave to the whims of those women from town, he probably gets an urge to sample one now and then. I imagine they don't always complain. Some urbanized women enjoy the occasional injection of uncouth nature. I'll check into Constant's comings and goings on the night of the events.

If I want to dismantle the mechanism now and identify the guilty party, I must beware of too much certainty. Everything must be questioned. Everything must raise absolute doubts.

Going back over my argument, I realize I

regard as certain the fact that the man in the closet didn't sign his crime — if, indeed, he committed one. That certainty is questionable. The assailant must have broken or moved some object, must have left behind a speck of dust, a fingerprint, a thread, a hair, a mark, a note, some cigarette ashes, a smell. I'll call the police chief.

"Hello, Chief. This is Barry Tremblay, the journalist. Sorry to bring this up, Chief, but you've got a reputation as a man who likes women, and there are some people who suspect you of what happened last night."

"That's slander! Malicious gossip! Lies! Or in other words, politics!"

"Nobody respects authority any more . . . Yes . . . Yes . . . I'm on your side. You were the first to arrive at the scene of the crime. Did you find any note from the assailant? A mark on a wall?"

"There was a letter in the bed of the girl who was attacked."

"Did you read the letter?"

"It was a fine envelope, fancy paper, and there was also a book and some magazines. It was a personal letter, I'm sure of that."

"If everyone who's fighting the war against crime thought like you, no criminals would ever be found."

"You said you were on my side."

"Chief, you've deprived us of the key to this whole business."

# CHAPTER 13

Of course Johanne was frightened, but aside from the broken window the house didn't suffer a scratch. Nicole Martin washed away the drops of blood. Constant replaced the window-pane. He had to: an October night isn't a night in June.

"Things like that never happen twice in a row," said Nicole Martin.

She and Pierre are back in the city. Tonight, the steak is properly cooked, rare, the way Pierre likes it. He doesn't dare compliment her on it. He's sensed all day that Nicole is about to spit fire. A cer-tain silence prevails in their Victorian house —

rather pretentious with its tacked-on turrets. The house of a successful family. A peaceful, opulent happiness dwells in it, they tell each other.

The cheese is good, as it so rarely is these days when merchants care less about their products than their profits. The wine? Isn't it a . . .

"Why such a good wine?" exclaims Pierre Martin. "Is this a special occasion?"

"At our age, every day is a special occasion," Nicole recites with exaggerated sweetness.

Something is up. Pierre becomes cautious.

"I'd gladly celebrate every day . . ."

"We're past the age for rolling in the grass like the colts at Lamontagne's farm in the spring. Anyway, we aren't colts . . ."

"What do you mean?"

Pierre sounded so blasé, surely his wife must have noticed. She knows he's hiding something. If that's the case, why not show some irritation?

"If you're trying to tell me something, go ahead, I'm no good at guessing!"

The traffic light that changes from green to yellow and then to red stains the chinks between the slats of the blind. The house is across from a park. Last year, a young cyclist was thrown and her doll run over by a truck. The residents of the street demanded a traffic light. It was Nicole Martin who organized the petition. Now the cars stop, but there's no escaping the coloured beams of light. Nicole Martin's face shifts from red to green. Pierre suspects that the red and the green also reflect her thoughts to some extent. What is this unavoidable storm that's brewing? Can it be held off for a while?

"Somebody stole Aubert's boat," Pierre announces nonchalantly.

"Everyone in that village gets their turn at being robbed."

"HIS boat. HIS shell. HIS cocoon. Aubert started building it a good eight or nine years ago. That boat's taken as long to build as Notre-Dame Cathedral in Paris."

"Notre Dame took more than eight or nine years," Nicole snaps.

"The thief has guts. You can't hide a boat like a wallet. It's big. A boat isn't a needle you can hide in a haystack."

"You can hide lots of things in a haystack."

Pierre wants to speak but he can't without stammering. For a moment he is open-mouthed, speechless. Finally he blurts out:

"When the Auberts got to their house they didn't notice the boat wasn't there."

"People don't always look carefully."

"It was only later that Aubert realized it was missing."

The pear tart is set down before him. The pears are almost cool, barely cooked. The cream is scented with kirsch.

"Didn't we agree to go on a diet?" asks Pierre.

"Let's just sample it. Isn't that one of your tenets, to sample things? I sample my dessert . . . and you . . ."

"Uhh . . . well, so do I," he says feebly.

Pierre wishes he were somewhere else. He can't escape.

Nicole brings out a bottle.

"Cognac too! I won't be able to concentrate on my work," he laments.

"I want to celebrate. Do you think those fingernail marks on your back are invisible? I'm divorcing you."

"What?"

"I'm divorcing you," she says again, slowly.

"But we've been together twenty-seven years, we have three children."

"I'm divorcing you. Pass the cognac."

Pierre's hand is shaking as he sets the bottle in front of her with exaggerated calm. His wife's hand almost touches his. He shivers. The warmth is familiar. Nicole pours a lot of cognac into her glass.

"I don't want to live with a man whose back is covered with scratches put there by another woman."

"If there are red marks on my back it's an allergy, you know that. I'm allergic to raspberries. I ate raspberries and cream yesterday."

"Liar."

She stares coldly into his eyes. Is she going to throw her glass at him? He gets ready to protect himself.

"You've been unfaithful."

"When a man's lived with a woman for so many years he can't really be unfaithful."

"I'm divorcing you. I could read a whole love poem on your back."

"A man needs a little distraction now and then, we both know that. Afterwards, he loves his wife even better."

"Go and live with your distraction. Your life with me is over. I'm divorcing you."

"That was yesterday. Yesterday is the past. I'd already forgotten. You're the one who reminded me of it. I didn't think about it afterwards. I didn't even think about it during!"

"She marked up your back like a roto-tiller! I'm divorcing you."

"I'll tell you everything. We aren't going to yell at each other like some poor, uneducated . . . I had a shock. I hit my head against the car door. In the ditch I was stunned. I may have been unconscious . . . I didn't dare tell you the rest . . . You wouldn't have understood."

"I'm divorcing you. I never believed in that ice on the road. For there to be ice there has to be water. And it hasn't rained for two days."

"The car spun like a top. It was a violent shock. Afterwards I felt as if I was dreaming. It was dark. I was lost in the countryside around Trois-Rivières. You know, along that highway there's nothing but lights blinking at the end of the plain. My car had its nose in the ditch. I didn't know whether to stay in the car or get out. I was talking it over with myself as if I were two or three people. I wanted someone to tell me what to do. I had no energy at all. I wanted to get out, but my arm muscles wouldn't open the door. I was in a kind of sleep where dream becomes reality.

"Finally I got out. There was too much night all around me. Everything was too far away. The night was a blue-black colour. I was stunned, quite simply knocked out. There was no blood, no pain, just a kind of inner ache. Would I wait? Would I walk? I was paralyzed in my torpor. All I could do was hesitate. I told myself: Maybe you'll have to wait till morning.

"I was in a daze.

"Suddenly a car pulled up. I wasn't sure of anything. When the car stopped I wasn't sure it was stopping. 'Get in . . .' It was a woman."

"That's a very roundabout way of telling me what I already know," says Nicole.

"She opened the car door for me. My arms were too limp. She said, 'You're lucky. You could be dead.'

"She drove me to her village. She opened the door of her house. It was warm. 'I'll fix you some herbal tea. Mint or lime-blossom? I'll look after you; after that we'll worry about your car. You see, my husband isn't here to help. He's with the Mounted Police. He's gone up north. It's been weeks since I've looked after a man.'"

"And she jumped on you to scratch your back . . ."

"What are you talking about? Under the impact when the car landed in the ditch, the springs in the seat shot out and left marks . . ."

"Liar! You're a filthy liar! Will you tell me how you got hay in your hair? Does the little lady from the Mounted Police keep a horse in her bedroom?"

"That's going too far . . . I don't intend to let . . ."

"Why did you write a cheque for fifteen hundred dollars yesterday, and to whom?"

"What! You've been snooping in my cheque-book! That's intolerable."

"My mother used to say, 'To find your man's heart, look in his cheque-book . . .' Pierre Martin, just go. I'll send your underwear and razor in the mail!"

# CHAPTER 14

This morning, the village curé is unable to celebrate Mass. The pious individuals who attend the ceremony every day to ready themselves for heavenly peace knock on a bolted door. They pull, push, pound. The solid doors stay shut.

"Constant had no right to go away and take the church keys," grumbles an irritated lady.

"Constant shouldn't attack the house of God," says an old lady with a faint beard.

"A man who attacks young girls at night could very well attack God Himself in the daytime," says a man bent by age.

Constant is responsible for the "sweeping, dusting, waxing and polishing of the church," according to his contract. To enable him to assume these responsibilities, the curé entrusted him with the keys to the church.

One day a new curé arrived with new ideas, "ecumenical" he called them. He believed that the faithful, not the priest, should hold the keys to the temple. The entire community decided that since Constant had already clipped onto his belt the keys for sweeping, dusting, waxing and polishing the church, it would be logical, fitting and useful for him to become the keeper of the ecclesiastical keys.

It's true, Constant was an immigrant from the next parish. He'd always been very different. This morning, people regretted having trusted Constant. They weren't surprised.

"Foreigners, they always go back where they came from," says one old man, his teeth clattering against his pipe.

"Those people don't give a hoot if we have to stand outside and freeze," says the former cobbler.

"He's treating us like we were foreigners, in our own church."

"He snuck away in the middle of the night, like a man that got caught doing something shameful."

"He ran away — that proves he's guilty."

"Yes, the man hiding in the closet was Constant!" declares the black widow who hasn't worn a coloured garment since her late husband's burial two hundred and forty-one months ago. "Constant has sin written across his face."

"Constant really liked being the handyman for those folks from town. It's understandable. There's at least one woman from town in every house. And Constant had a liking for them."

"Those foreigners, they understand each other."

Constant has, quite simply, disappeared. He didn't think it over very long. A noise wakened him up. Another noise. Broken glass. His bedroom window shattered. Glass was crumbling in another bedroom too. A brick landed in his bed. He grabbed his pants, pulled them on. It wasn't easy with the crutches . . .

Fear choked him. His breathing sounded like that of another person in his bedroom. Constant didn't dare switch on the light, expose himself. He listened. There was nothing outside on the street except the night. Yet rocks were hitting his house. Stones bounced off his bedroom wall and rolled along the floor.

Suddenly a voice cried out: "Rapist!"

Another window shattered. It was time to run.

Norbert is Constant's neighbour. There's no love lost between them, everyone knows that. Their houses stand face-to-face, on either side of the main street. Each man spies on the other, everyone knows that. In both houses, the front windows are covered by opaque blinds. In each blind, however, as everybody knows, there is a little hole for observing the other man.

If Barry Tremblay, the journalist, wants to learn anything about Constant, Norbert's the man to ask, he thinks.

"In connection with recent events involving a man in a closet and two young girls in the house on the Gentle Rise Road, did you notice anything across from your house?"

Norbert looks the journalist square in the eye, appraising him. He pulls out his pipe, taps it against his hand. He fishes a knife from his pocket to scrape the bowl. He stows his knife and his pipe in the inside pocket of his jacket. He slips off his glasses, wipes them on his handkerchief, hooks them onto his nose again. His movements are solemn. This ceremony heralds an important declaration.

"You see," says Norbert, aiming his gaze at the journalist's eyes, "Constant's the only man in the village that has access to the Martins' house. When a person's got the keys he doesn't need to bash the door in. I'd swear on a stack of Bibles, Constant went to see those two girls staying at the

Martins'. Any place there's a woman, it attracts Constant. He can smell them from far away. Come Saturday and Sunday, Constant's as happy as a devil in Hell. All the women are back. He'll go down to the cellar with one to fix some pipes. He'll go up to the attic with another to beef up the insulation. He'll fix one woman's bed, he's in the barn with another. Constant's the king of those creatures.

"Constant's like a dog, he needs stroking. And the women from town know where he likes it. Constant knows those women pretty well, but he knows their men, too. Now, where nature's concerned, those men from town are a little feeble. Constant, though, he's as full of vice as a stallion. Constant's always had a feeling for women. He came here from the next parish. A total stranger. Before the dust of our village was on his boots he was already making eyes at our women. Nobody even knew his name and already he was after our women. He wasn't bald back then; he'd take his cap off when he saw you on the street. His face wasn't all shrivelled up like an old apple. He had a smile like butter on a slice of warm bread. He still had all his teeth. Women, they're the way they are; they got a soft spot for a stranger.

"My own sweetheart, she was bewitched by that gypsy. We had our plans for the future. We were talking about marriage. She belonged to me. Then Constant arrived. With no respect for vows of love, he took away my sweetheart . . . And then he married her. Leaving me high and dry, so to speak. I was the laughing-stock of the town. After that happened, I could never get myself elected mayor or town councillor or churchwarden. I could never walk down the main street with my soul at rest. I knew there was always somebody thinking: 'Look, here comes Norbert, the man whose wife was stolen by Constant.'

"Now, I'm a man that doesn't let bad luck get him down. I found another woman who agreed to marry the man whose wife was stolen by Constant. She gave me nine children. I was as happy as a man can be. There wasn't a day I didn't think: the woman that was supposed to be my wife is in Constant's house. He steals other men's women. He was like that when he was young. And he's like that in his old age.

"Constant had the key to the Martins' house. He went in without making a sound. His crutches have learned how to be pretty sneaky. He's right at home in other people's houses. He waited till the time was right to come out of that closet. He waited till the girl had her clothes off. Constant's always hankered after women that belong to other men.

"Now I don't tell tales, but with my house right across from his house, I know what I know. And since you asked, on the night of the rape

Constant went out in his car. With the lights off. He didn't want to be seen. I saw what I saw.

"His poor late wife must be crying up there in Heaven, where she can see what her husband's up to. She must regret the error of her life: marrying him instead of me. Take fingerprints. You'll find Constant's fingers on the actress's body.

"And now this morning, at the church, Constant's preventing Christians from practising their religion. He's got the keys, so he figures that gives him all the rights."

"Thank you," says the young journalist, "I only wanted to check the facts."

# CHAPTER 15

Will I ever be able to sleep again? wonders Johanne, the actress. Will I be able to forget that a door can open suddenly in the night? Will I be able to get to sleep without blocking the closet door with a trunk or a chest of drawers? Will I be able to sleep where there's a window without iron bars? Will I have to keep a revolver on my bedside table? Will I be able to sleep without being terrified by the nightmare of a man who can pass through walls? Will I ever be able to watch night approach without fearing that a man is hiding there? What a fright I must have had, to throw myself naked through a window. What a fright!

Standing here, motionless, I look at the cedars in the valley below. They glitter in the wintry air. If I could bring back my fear, exactly the way it felt then, I would scream like a torture victim, and then I'd hurl myself out a window again. When I think about it my breathing changes: there's less air. As he hid in the night, that man was panting as he thought of crucifying me on my mattress. I wish I could vomit the air I inhaled with him!

I'm condemned to fear the night. That terror won't leave me. I'll no longer be able to enjoy the quiet happiness that comes at the end of the day. Night will be the black hour when someone can burst out and assault me. Never again will I be able to gaze out at the night and think: "Some of God's mystery has come and touched down on Earth." No, instead I'll fear that one of Creation's errors, a monster, a rutting male, will leap out at me.

And yet I've long been acquainted with fear. I borrow the lives of my characters — am I afraid of the person I am? When I'm in the skin of characters who aren't me, I feel reassured.

Unless I'm on a stage or in front of cameras I'm afraid of people's looks. When someone's eyes are on me they feel like hands that are pulling my clothes off. Why don't I have the right to walk down the street like a cat without a care in the world? Why does that lid of fear always cover me? I know . . . I'm a desirable woman, or so people tell me. It would be a pretentious thing to say if I weren't so afraid of being desirable. Desirable: it's what I try not to be. I want to be just a woman. A woman has enough reasons to be afraid. She doesn't need to be desirable, too.

When I was little, I was afraid of my father's fat cheeks. When he sat me on his knees I was afraid of his big hairy hands on my thighs when he squeezed them with his fat brown fingers. I was afraid of his breath filled with tobacco smoke. I was afraid of his big arms that crushed me. I was afraid of his big hard hairy chest where I could feel his heart pounding away. Even though he died years ago, sometimes I can still hear his big heart pounding. If it happens at night, I'm afraid. And I think about those big invisible arms that could squeeze me and shatter me like an eggshell.

In my child's bed I was afraid when my mother put out the light. I'd close my eyes so I wouldn't see the night. It wasn't the "achromatic night" of the poet whose work I read on national radio, it was pitch-black night my small body was afraid of falling into, a bottomless hole that is never touched by daylight. How frightened I was!

Now when I close my eyes I'm still afraid of falling. That bad memory is in my soul forever.

I play happy roles, but I'm afraid of being in the world. I bite deeply into life, as they say; that's because I'm afraid! I still don't understand why this life has to end. I still haven't understood how deep is the hole that opens when we close our eyes forever. Yet I'm a tough young woman too. I walk alone in the city late at night. I never turn my head when I hear footsteps behind me. I turn into the subway and go where I'm going. I don't tremble when I'm waiting for a taxi. I've learned how to live with my fear. I've put to sleep the fear of the little girl who was launched into a world too big for her, where there are too many questions with no answers.

Each role gives me a companion I can live with for as long as I play that part. I forget my fears a little as I devote myself to hers.

All those fears I've accumulated, made powerless, held in check, were unleashed when that closet door opened, slowly, almost without a sound.

When I was a child, my fear was a profound intuition about life. A woman is born fully prepared for the fear she'll experience.

I live as women do: I pretend that I'm not afraid.

# CHAPTER 16

CHAPTER 16

The clouds glide above the forest amid a muffled silence. In the house, people fall silent and listen to the mutter of logs in the fire. Charlotte says to Johanne:

"I want to talk about that letter you found in your bed. There's something so dramatic about a letter after an attack: it may have blood on it, or fingerprints. You did the right thing, you know, giving it to me."

"You took it!" Johanne corrects her.

"That letter could turn out to be damaging evidence," Charlotte points out.

"I know. If you haven't burnt it, it'll lead us to

the man in the closet. It's proof of the crime . . .
The attacker . . . My letter explains the mystery."

"You said 'my' letter again. What makes you
think it's yours?"

"Because I found it in my bed."

"And you think," Charlotte taunts her,
pouting, "you think that while the man was in that
closet he took time out to write you a letter before
he put in his appearance?"

"It was in my bed! It was, it was intended for
me."

Johanne gazes at Charlotte, her eyes suddenly wide with horror, the horror of having been
deceived.

"You had no right to burn it!"

She throws herself at her friend, who does
not shrink back. The two fall and roll across the
floor. Johanne scratches, hits, screams, clutches.
Charlotte accepts the blows without returning
them.

Gradually Johanne calms down, extricating
her limbs from her friend's and staying there
beside her on the carpet, silent, weeping. Charlotte too has tears running down her temple.

"Tell me," Johanne pleads, "why don't you
want the guilty person exposed?"

"Listen," Charlotte insists, "listen to me. That
letter wasn't for you. It was for me. Yes, I took it
from you. I don't want the person who wrote it
accused of being the man in the closet."

"It was in my bed."

"Do you remember," murmurs Charlotte once her breathing is normal again, "when I went to see the dressmaker? You didn't want to come, remember? You just wanted to sit on the balcony, wrapped in blankets like an onion in its skin. Remember? I love walking. In the fall there's no perfume but the perfume of the air. You feel as if you're breathing air from above the clouds.

"So I was walking, by myself as you know, a little dazed — a little drunk, if you want. A car came along. I moved over to the shoulder. The car slowed down. I was afraid. I'm sick of being a woman! Goddamn our fear! Why can't a woman take a walk under the good Lord's sky without being afraid? I heard my name. I was even more afraid. Then I recognized the driver. It was Pierre Martin!"

"What was he doing on the Gentle Rise Road?" exclaimed Johanne.

"I asked him that. 'I felt like seeing you,' he answered. 'Seeing *me*?' I repeated. I've often caught him giving me a sweet, sad look that changes as soon as his wife is there. His wife and I are like aunt and niece. Pierre and Nicole love Italy. When they went there, they lent me their house. Pierre has often told me: 'I want you to know, if you bring a man there, I'll be very jealous. And if you don't turn my picture around I'll be watching you!' When they came home Pierre saw that I'd done so and he found a way to put it back while I was there, with a knowing smile, as if he really had been watching me."

"Tell me, Charlotte, is there anything between Pierre and you?"

"There wasn't anything. We were like Joseph and Mary . . . Yesterday, when Pierre's car came along, slowing down, its lights blinding me, I was frightened . . ."

"Men and women will never be equal; women will always be more frightened than men."

"I'm not afraid of any man, goddammit! I've gone up to a few men, even at night. I've travelled in many countries. Sometimes on dark and narrow streets . . . Luckily it was Pierre.

" 'Do you know why I'm here?' he asked with a shy smile, not really daring to look at me with his little eyes. 'No, I don't know.' With that adorable, shy little smile he said, 'I came to ask you something I've been wanting to ask for a long time. I've never dared . . . I've never dared to ask because I was afraid . . . I was afraid you'd say no!' Like I said, I was scared, a little dazed, I didn't grasp the innuendoes, the non-verbal message. My intuitive radar was scrambled. Pierre went on: 'I drove a hundred and sixty kilometres and I kept telling myself: There's practically no chance of meeting Charlotte. If I do meet her, it's a sign. And now I've met you.' I chided him: 'My Lord, you're mysterious! What is it you want to ask me?' 'I want to make love to you. I've wanted you for years.'

"I felt like laughing in his face, turning it into a joke, teasing poor Pierre, but it wasn't a laugh or a smile that came to my lips; I said, 'Yes.' I felt myself going red. I got into his car. Then we thought of the same thing that country school-children think of. We went and had our fun in the hay in that old stable, you know, by the curve. Pierre's an adolescent. Making love in a haystack!"

"How was it?"

"Pierre even brought blankets! He cried on my shoulder like a big baby."

"That's so sweet!"

"He promised to take me sailing in the South Seas. As he was leaving, he gave me a letter that he said expressed his deepest feelings.

"When I came back to the house, remember, you said: 'The dressmaker certainly took her time!'

"Then the phone rang. I was next to your bedroom and I ran to pick up the phone on your bedside table. The letter must have slipped from my hands . . . And then with everything that happened, I forgot it."

# CHAPTER 17

Paradise was jolted by an earthquake whose epicentre was the Martins' closet. To go and check on the damage, each person left office, university, client, meeting, operation. There they were, in the middle of the week, outside their country houses as if it were Saturday.

They don't go inside right away. First, the male circles the fortress. Are there footprints around the house? Has the grass been trampled? Are tire tracks printed on the gravel? Is there a broken window? Has the ladder leaning against the wall been moved? Everything looks normal. The male decides to go inside. The woman will wait for him to emerge. Has the lock been forced? The male inspects the premises: bedrooms, basement. Every closet is visited.

The families are relieved to have been spared this time. When will their turn come? The man in the closet hasn't caught his victim, he'll be back. This time, they'll know how to welcome him. Defence systems are put in place: here a rifle, there a stick. Procedures are established: women will go to bed only if a male is present. Don't lift the covers before you look under the bed and behind the curtains; don't forget to check the lock on the window; above all, inspect the closet.

Then all these people meet on their way to the general store or the bank. They chat.

"One thing's certain: two attractive girls are even more attractive deep in the woods."

"If they're attractive, no one should be surprised if they attract!"

"So many men nowadays have no backbone, no guts, no balls; I respect a man who likes women."

"There's a way to go about it . . ."

"Every normal man enjoys the hunt."

"When I look at what they call the new men (you know the kind I mean, a baby-sitter with a mouth full of diaper pins and hands covered in flour), I take off my hat to any man who'd dare to break into a house and wait for the woman he desires."

"Hearing talk like that in the twentieth century makes me sick to my stomach!"

"There's always somebody to justify humiliating a woman."

Finally, everyone feels obliged to go and comfort the two victims of the Gentle Rise Road. They're both there, rather like strangers in the midst of these people who see one another every weekend, who talk about them as if they were someone else. Johanne and Charlotte sit on a love-seat and listen.

"I deciphered the information but I found nothing significant. It's a non-event. A non-event that contains non-significance. Rather than apply a non-philosophy to a non-event, the few thoughtful intelligences in this part of the country should instead formulate hypotheses for real events that will engage the essence of the individual."

When the writer deposits his Cuban cigarillo on the edge of the table and his beer glass on the carpet between his feet, people listen. He gesticulates. Any moment now, the feet will follow the hands. The beer glass will receive a kick that will send it flying. He will be forgiven. He's a genius. During the week he carves up his fictional sausage on national TV. Weekends, he creates pure poetry by spilling boxes of alphabet noodles onto the floorboards. A visiting Parisian reckoned that "his poetry is more than poetry, for it contains the essence of sculpture." Since then, you can find his name in the arts section of the city newspaper. After listening to the writer, no one can forgive himself for having worried about a non-event.

"Where are the Martins . . .?"

"The killer never returns to the scene of the crime!"

"What a terrible thing to say!"

"They've phoned several times," Johanne points out. "They were the first to come, and then they left."

"So the Martins went out of their way for a non-event . . ."

"Pierre's quite fond of women. And they tend to reciprocate. If I'd been Pierre, with two beautiful women in my own house, my own bed, and if I was a little weary of my wife, I'd have jumped at the chance to get a little glimpse of young rear-end."

"You're a dirty old man!"

"I'm only taking advantage of Pierre's absence! Of course old Pierre is goodness and kindness personified. Even if he'd been tempted by the devil's magic potion, he'd have resisted."

The jokes, the verbiage irritate Johanne. For these idle city people, talk replaces thought.

"Maybe one of you is the man in the closet!" she challenges.

And she runs and hides in her room. The visitors are surprised at her mood. But they understand.

"Nevertheless, Pierre Martin was seen in the area on the night of the non-event."

"Pierre would have been here to see us," Charlotte pleads. "We were treated very well. I'm very fond of him. And I want any cynics to know, if Pierre came on to me, I'd say yes. And so would the rest of you women! Pierre's a charming, seductive man. Conclusion: Pierre Martin had no need to hide in a closet!"

Suddenly, an angel passes, as they say in the village. Conversations trail off. Everyone starts to think about going home.

The police chief will have the last word. As both chief and sole employee of the village police force, what could he have done to prevent all these misdeeds? Thieves are like lightning: they strike once, then they fade away. They break a window, force a lock, grab a few dollars, some jewellery, tools, clothes, knick-knacks, appliances, then they take off. Disappear without leaving a trace or an address, then return to work in the fall when the summer people migrate back to town. How can the chief of police, all by himself, keep an eye on every house? These city people perch in the woods where even the moon can't see them. If they've built out in the open, they'll hide their bungalow behind bushes they bring in the trunks of their cars.

The police chief isn't the all-seeing God. He's

snowed under. What's more, the mayor has asked him to spread sand so his wife won't slip on the ice like a hen when she walks to church. He can't do everything. Besides, these break-and-enters didn't exist before the invasion of those fancy folks from town. The other day, a thief gave himself a treat: to avoid the trouble of bashing in a door he took a power-saw and cut a hole in a wall. The police chief heard the noise. It was the middle of the day. He thought nothing of it. Here and there, farmers were sawing their wood. He can't see everything. "Let those city people build along the road like everybody else if they want me to see their houses!" It's very strange: it's only the fancy folks from town who get robbed. If they weren't here, there'd be no robberies in the village!

So speaks the chief of police as he heads for the Martin house. It's planted in the middle of the forest, as if they were afraid of the civilized world. He pounds his fist on the door. Probably the two young ladies have barricaded themselves inside. They must be worried about the man in the closet coming back. The echo of his fists travels up towards the mountains. At last, someone comes. It's no life, being snowed under all the time.

"Police!" he announces.

"I can see that," says the woman who has deigned to let him in, the one who's not the actress.

The other one comes to join her. The actress. The one who was attacked and who jumped through a window.

"Have you found the guilty party?"

"No."

"I'd have been surprised if you had," says the other girl, who always seems to know what's going to happen next week.

The chief has spotted her several times before, when she was visiting the Martins.

"I protect the whole village by myself. I'm snowed under. There've been death threats. Stones thrown at Constant's windows. They're stoning him like Mary Magdalene, the woman taken in sin. According to public opinion, he's the man that was waiting in your closet. Poor Constant took to his heels, took off with his crutches . . . I'm just back from the Standing Rock Stream. Fat Ferdinande had a rifle to the forehead of her Benjamin, who was huddling in a corner. Ferdinande was ready to blow his brains out. She claims it was her man in your closet. She found a woman's hair on his lumberjack shirt. He came in late last night. There was something different about him. She could even smell a woman's perfume. I'm snowed under. Because of that closet of yours, ladies, everybody's guilty. Seems like those that aren't wish they were! I've heard with my own eardrums, I've heard some fellows say: 'If the man in the closet missed those two females, guess I'll go and try my luck.' Since that's the situation, ladies, I'm giving you a municipal order to leave our boundaries immediately. I'm snowed under, I can't guarantee your safety."

# CHAPTER 18

Barry Tremblay is writing his news bulletin for the local radio station. The local newspaper. The local news. A local career. A local life. A local death . . . NO!

One day, he'll get out of here. One day he will soar as high as the stars. One day, he will work for a real radio station, write for a real newspaper. He will unmask the man in the closet. How the local people will be relieved! He has gathered all the facts. Now all that's left is to connect them by a logical link.

A bad joke drifts into his mind: the man will come out of the closet and Barry Tremblay will come out of his hole!

Who doesn't have in his house a wife, a sister, a cousin, a friend? Who doesn't have a closet? Everyone is worried. Everyone feels threatened. His story will touch the crowd. Barry Tremblay will become a known name, a familiar voice, perhaps a famous face. Not everything is negative. This godforsaken hole where he's working himself to death is the backstage of the great theatre where he awaits his turn to go on stage.

He is having trouble concentrating. Isn't it time to set aside the man in the closet and write his item for the ten o'clock news?

An idiotic truck-driver has been arrested at the American border. The company he works for is well known. The northern highway runs beside the lot where his trucks are parked.

At the customs station the officer asked him:

"What are you transporting?"

"A boat. Can't you see?"

"Where are you taking this boat?"

"To Florida. It's a fine place for a boat. It's hot, you can wear your bathing suit, and there's water!"

"Does this boat belong to you?"

"I wish it did, but you need plenty of cash to have a boat like this."

"Do you have the ownership papers?"

"I left in a hurry."

"Pull over to the right."

That was when the trucker realized he was a character in a peculiar story. He suspected nothing. He should have.

Barry Tremblay is struggling with his lead paragraph. It's always the hardest one.

Local trucker Robert Lebel has been apprehended at the U.S. border. After a close investigation, customs officials accused him of theft. With no owner-ship papers, he was transporting to Florida a boat that did not belong to him.

Once you've started, it's enough not to stop.

The actual owner of the boat, Dr. Aubert, a city-dweller who maintains a secondary residence in our village, had already reported the boat's disappear-ance to police.

Denying any guilt or collusion in the matter, trucker Lebel gave the fol-lowing account: The previous day, a rather tall man had asked if he could transport his boat to Florida. Lebel was not available. When the man told how much he would pay, Lebel changed his mind. The man wrote him a generous cheque as an advance. Then both men went to see the boat and assess the work required. It was late in the evening, but the man was educated and distinguished. Lebel suspected nothing. The two shook hands. The man said: "I'll be in Florida before you. If everything works out, you'll get a bonus."

Lebel was quite obviously, and quite naively, acting in good faith.

It was a simple matter to track down the person responsible for the theft. The protagonist in this fantastic tale is the architect Pierre Martin.

Finally, Barry Tremblay observes once again, it's almost hard to stop writing.

What was the motive behind this preposterous act of soft-water piracy? Why would a happily married, professionally successful man steal a friend's boat, when he has the means to buy himself an entire fleet? Perhaps a woman's presence in this story would explain his peculiar behaviour. Martin gave trucker Lebel the impression he could no longer tolerate the Canadian winter.

"Too literary," the journalist decided. "How can I translate that into local radio language?"

While he is wasting his time, the man from the closet is still at large.

# CHAPTER 19

The two young women cannot forgive themselves for allowing themselves to be expelled. Why didn't they resist? The municipal police chief said: "We're clearing out the house!" Like two well-brought-up, obedient young ladies, they obeyed and started cramming their clothes into their suitcases. Now they are in the car. They are driving back to the city. They are furious.

"They threw us out like garbage. Shit! And we didn't say a word!"

"There was no reason for us to go. They cut short our good life in the country."

"The house is empty and we're on the highway."

"We were as silent as nuns."

"Contemplative nuns of St. Phallus. Goddammit! This is the twentieth century, with all its ideological and moral revolutions, all the taboos overthrown, but a man tells us 'You've got no business here' and we listen, say 'Thank you' and go away. Goddammit! To hell with obedience!"

"Look at me, I yell my head off to make my living, but my lips were sealed. Total silence. The obedient virgin. Bowing and scraping to the father. Goddammit, I hate myself!"

"Let's go back."

"Goddammit! I hate it when I humiliate myself like that."

"Let's go back."

"Even if they found out today that a woman invented the wheel, we still wouldn't have our revenge!"

In the half-light, one can see sparks in the other's eyes. Rage. Humiliation. Compliance, which they reject. Johanne is driving. She says again:

"Let's go back."

"I'll only go back to that dump to become mayor and fire their useless police chief. That's the way to treat them: become boss and make them whimper for their security like they whimpered and moaned for their mothers' milk."

"You're hard . . ."

"When the men are soft, you have to be!"

The road is straight, with long, cautious curves. The night is pitch-black. The only stars are those in the eyes of the two girls. The night is pure. The north wind is sharp. No fog. Headlight beams travel a long distance. A deer could show itself, fascinated by the light. One must be attentive. Ready to apply the brakes. In the distance, the villages already look a little like Christmas.

At this time of year one shouldn't be surprised if snow starts falling. But they are surprised — a little, a lot. In no time the windshield has fogged up like spectacles. The flakes flatten into big white drops. The snow accumulates. The wipers aren't fast enough. They have to slow down. They can't see heaven or earth, not even the night on the other side of the windshield. The actress grips the wheel. Slows down. The windshield wipers race. Snow falls.

"The snow is so beautiful," says Charlotte. "We could be in our house instead of out here in the fields — with a fire in the fireplace, crackling maple logs, something to smoke, something to drink . . ."

"That man in the closet scared me. Scared me like when I was little. It was the devil, the fire, I don't know."

The flakes are fat. Their eyes don't grow accustomed to them. The windshield wipers are doing their job. Now the road is painted white. No cars ahead of them. Behind them, no headlights.

They have to talk now because they're together. They have to talk because it's dark. Words create a certain brightness. They must talk because the snow is silent. They must talk because they have something to say to each other and because perhaps it's better to say it in the dark. Begin by talking about the snow? That would be nice. You feel a pang when winter suddenly lets down its white hair. You think of the little girl you used to be, in your pink snowsuit trimmed with fur. You remember being a teenager on skates, skating with the first boy who put his arm around your waist. The snow is fascinating. Somewhat hypnotizing. The car seems to have stopped moving. Millions of white butterflies, barely moving their wings, are flying towards you. There are so many; you're dazed. The snow hangs a curtain. Unable now to see the earth, you look inside your soul.

"You shouldn't have been so afraid of the man in the closet."

"And you should have been in my shoes. 'Shouldn't have been so afraid...' When a man jumps on me in the night, without being invited..."

Despite herself, her hands have moved the wheel. For a moment, the car hesitates. Will they go to the left, to the right?

"See, I'm still afraid. That was my nerves reacting. I can't see anything with this snow. We're stopping at the next motel, even if we're almost back in town. This is an avalanche!"

"Okay. The motel's on me."

"I can pay my share," says the actress, "I leased my smile to the mayonnaise company, remember."

"Johanne, this snow inspires me. I'm going to share some secrets with you. All these snowflakes are making me giddy. Johanne, I'm in love."

"You mean, really in love?"

"Yes. A lot more than I think. A lot more than you think."

"With Pierre?"

"Don't be crazy!" She laughs.

Let's move cautiously now. Let's go more slowly. The sky seems to be releasing all the snow predicted for the winter. The white butterflies are flattening against the windshield like real butterflies in summer; finally it looks messy. It's colder, too. The windshield wipers are applying an icy skin as they push away the snow.

"Now it's freezing," the actress complains.

"Can you believe it, Johanne, I still remember the first time I saw you in a play, in your French maid's apron. All the other actors were on stage, even the great . . . what's his name? He sounded as if he thought he was being paid by the syllable. You didn't have much to do, but you were . . . you were the one I watched. A few weeks later, I saw you on TV. I remember exactly what you were selling: some hair-care product. Can you believe it? I went out and bought some. It's the brand I still use. You'll see. Haven't you noticed it in my bathroom? Then I saw you on stage again. You didn't have much to do, but you have a way of asserting your presence. As if you're saying, 'Life! Here I am!' I tried to find what restaurant your group had gone to. I arranged to talk to you."

"I remember. When I came home from our European tour I was surprised to see you. We hadn't known each other very long. It's always nice to see a familiar face at the airport. I was glad."

"I was intimidated, myself."

"It's clearing up. I can see better."

They can drive faster now. The actress has a firm grip on the wheel. The car leaves two straight, parallel tracks. Ahead of them, in the night, headlights pick out the road. The first flakes have melted on contact with the asphalt. An icy film has formed under the snow. They're aware of it. The tires have lost their traction. Johanne is driving steadily. She's driving well. She's driving straight ahead. She is expected back in town shortly.

"Constant said my car's dangerous . . . It drives as if it was brand new . . . He was probably looking for work!"

"Johanne," says Charlotte, "I'm very much in love. I'm going to do something stupid."

"I wish you'd tell me who it is that's got you in such a state."

"Johanne, were you really afraid of the man in the closet?"

"Yes. My heart was in my mouth!"

"I feel so terrible. The last thing I wanted was to frighten you!"

"What?"

"I only wanted to touch your hair, kiss your forehead, I don't know what . . ."

"What! You're out of your mind! Or worse! It was you!"

Is it possible? She can't believe it. She remembers. She's amazed. Incredulous. The road is slippery. She forgets that she is driving.

Too late. In Johanne's nervous hands the wheel has slipped. She applies the brakes, jerks the wheel to one side, the other, to straighten out the car. It skates, dances, glides, then skids to the shoulder. What a swerve! The car rolls down. It is deep.

A little later, a truck with powerful headlights stops. The driver takes out a flashlight and goes down to inspect the damage. The car has overturned and landed on its roof. It's completely crumpled. No tracks around it. People are still inside. He calls. The car is wedged tight in the ditch. He sees blood. What a mess inside! Long

hair. Girls? Boys? You never know nowadays . . .
Fingernails. Women's fingernails. They mustn't
have fastened their seat belts.

"Young people nowadays don't accept con-
straints. They want to be free . . ."

The truck-driver mutters as he climbs back
up the escarpment:

"Back when women looked after the house
instead of going off in a snowstorm, these acci-
dents didn't happen. More children that won't be
born because there won't be a mother for them!"

Down below, in the ditch, the actress and her
friend hold each other tight. For all eternity, one
will be in love and the other will not understand.

# CHAPTER 20

Would Barry Tremblay be condemned to perish in this godforsaken hole? At his mirror, he loathes himself. His face is not unpleasant, nor his eyes, but he hates something in himself that's not reflected in the glass: a kind of sluggishness, an inertia that holds him back. He's always too late.

If he had unmasked the man in the closet, he'd have won some journalistic kudos. He could have got a job with a real newspaper in the city. He investigated, verified the rumours, reconstituted the comings and goings of several suspects. He assembled all the pieces of the puzzle, he managed to put them together. Only two were left: the girls. He had to question them. They had agreed to see him.

Barry Tremblay was subjected to some tight negotiations, conducted by the lawyer. She insisted on approving the photograph of the actress. She demanded that the picture be run across at least five columns of the front page. This issue of *L'Écho du royaume du Nord* would be sent to every daily in the country. Finally, Barry Tremblay had to agree that the first half of the published interview would deal with the incident of the man in the closet, the second with the actress's career.

Several times, Barry Tremblay almost let slip: "Your actress isn't Marilyn Monroe yet."

He restrained himself. He was as silent as a sphinx who asks the prerequisite questions through which each person reveals and betrays himself.

Barry Tremblay was convinced that the two would help him escape from the village. His confidence was unshakable: he would penetrate the mystery of those strange nocturnal movements in an isolated country house.

The two girls had fled before he saw them. He arrived at the meeting at the appointed time. Too late. They had already disappeared.

In a flash, one fact illuminated the scene. The girls had run away, and so they held the key to the enigma. That was his conclusion. He immediately contacted the municipal police chief.

"They've vanished into thin air. The guilty party never remains at the scene of the crime," he insinuated.

"When young people are foolish, they're really foolish!" retorted the chief of police. "They left because I ordered them to leave."

That was all. Barry Tremblay's entire enterprise crumbled. His dream of escape, his dream of the future, was over. He lit a cigarette. His dream, he mused, hadn't even left any ash. He'd been born in this hole, did he have to die here too?

Then the news arrived: on the way to the city, the car with the actress and the lawyer had taken a tragic swerve. At once, he phoned the chief of municipal police:

"You're the one," he charged, "who pushed them into the storm. Will you accept responsibility for this fatal tragedy?"

"It's not the facts that interest you, it's politics. So you do it at my expense, you attack justice, shake up law and order . . . One of these days I'm going to padlock that lying computer of yours. You want to criticize the legal system but you can't even get the price of peas right in your newspaper. There was a mistake again last week. Georgianna caught it."

One day, Barry Tremblay would be free. That morning, he was still a slave of his rag. Unable to follow the Ariadne thread that led back to the man in the closet, and with no established facts, he decided to wax lyrical. For many readers, emotions are enough. Since Barry Tremblay had been unable to make people notice him through his acute analyses and rigorous reasoning, his final recourse would be his poetic style. In the world of journalism, where style seems to have been flattened under the vast weight of the presses, he thinks, his own would appear unique.

FIERY DRAMA IN THE SNOW! Yesterday, the snow wept. Stars became tears. The sorrowing sky bowed before the bodies of two young girls, victims of the highway as others have been victims of the battlefield.

Earlier this week, the same young girls had cried out in the night. As one of them was getting into bed, suddenly, in the silence, a closet door trembled and creaked, then was flung open and the young girl was attacked.

Who committed the crime of profaning the solitude of a young girl in her bed?

Rumour has it that the man in the closet was the guilty party.

No one saw his face. No one recognized the shape of his body.

No one has discovered his tracks.

Poor dead young girls, in your coffin of battered metal beneath the weeping snow, you know full well that your assailant was death. Invisible, without footprints or fingerprints, death came to breathe the perfume of life from your bodies, then swallowed you up in his huge black maw with its rumblings of eternity.

Barry Tremblay re-read himself several times, just for pleasure. He made a correction here, an adjustment there. Satisfied, he did not finish his article, he abandoned it, in the words of the poet Paul Valéry that he'd pinned to his lampshade.

It was time to leave. The architect Pierre Martin, buccaneer of the Gentle Rise Road, who had stolen the Auberts' boat, was to appear before the regional court.

It wasn't Pierre who turned up before the judge but Nicole, his wife.

"His ex-wife. I've divorced him. I don't want to hear another word about him. I lived with him for twenty-seven years and now I don't want to count those years in my age. Let him give me half of our property, then disappear as if he'd never existed. I want to hate him, to erase the love I made the mistake of feeling for him in the past.

He didn't deserve that love. He doesn't deserve my hate. Your Honour, I've come in his place because my ex-husband is too ashamed. You can't impose so much shame on a man. He's prepared to pay for everything: the trucker to return the boat to our friends the Auberts, the legal costs, even the rental of the boat. He's prepared to pay compensation. He's prepared to buy the boat if he has to. He's prepared to pay whatever is necessary to erase his error. Dr. Aubert specializes in diseases of the soul. He will understand my husband — my former husband."

Dr. Aubert blows his nose hard, then says *sotto voce*:

"Pierre Martin tried to steal my dream. There's no price for my dream. I want to see Pierre Martin before a judge, with handcuffs on his wrists."

The day after the accident, Constant was discovered in his car. Everything seemed clear. Constant had taken his own life. The man in the closet had meted out the punishment he deserved, or so the village decided.

Constant had no family. He didn't have a single friend, even though he'd spent his entire life in this place. It was decided that he must be buried straightaway.

He had not died a Christian death. And so he was not entitled to a Christian burial. Through his deed, Constant had overstepped the will of God. Thus he had denied himself the cemetery that is the resting place of those who live and die as Christians.

"Perhaps the people in his native parish should look after him?" someone suggested. "They're the ones who are really responsible for Constant."

"We only put up with him," explained Norbert. "They're the ones that made him the way he was."

There was relief in the village at the sight of the ambulance disappearing on the other side of the hill, at the boundary of the village. Constant was returning whence he came.

Before he died, Constant had wanted to go to confession because he had committed a grave offence. It was so grave, he hadn't wanted to kneel before the parish priest. Instead, he decided to speak to God Himself.

Constant made sure that both the garage door and the window were tightly shut. Then he got into his car and closed the door. He took off his cap. Usually he didn't even take it off to sleep. He gazed at his face in the rear-view mirror like someone who wants to remember, later. And he turned the ignition key. The engine purred. Constant had just replaced the oil.

"God," he began, "I loved those two girls and I've committed a mortal sin. Forgive me. You didn't give me much intelligence and I made bad use of what you gave me. Maybe it was a blessing that you gave me so little. If I'd had more intelligence, perhaps I'd have done more wrong.

"Those two young creatures meant a lot to me. With their beauty and vitality they lit a fire in my old body. They're high-spirited. They're made of flesh. They love life. And happiness. They love love and they know how to love. They walk through the world like free beings. In my day, women went through life like they were going to a funeral. You didn't make life sad like that, God! Beautiful girls like them aren't interested in an old man like me.

"The other day they asked me to put on their winter tires. They talked to me while I was working. With their little ways, their teasing, they made me feel young enough to do anything, even with my crutches. Just when I was feeling so happy, though, a sadness came to my soul. I thought: After I've finished my job I won't see those girls again.

"The car was up on the jack. I slid underneath and I loosened the safety bolt at the joint in the drive shaft. I thought, the worst that can happen is the girls will lose control and land in the ditch on the Martins' lane.

"I warned them: 'Your drive shaft looks to me to be in bad shape. Drive very slowly. Here in the country it isn't dangerous. There's not much traffic. Especially on the Gentle Rise Road. But don't go beyond it.'

"I was sure they'd leave their car and ask me to fix it. Dear God, I'd have come to their rescue like a shot!

"When I didn't hear anything, I told myself I'd come back and tighten that bolt before they got on the highway. And that's the truth, God.

"I'm a lonely, unhappy old man who killed two beautiful girls who created happiness just as you, God, created the sun. It was a terrible sin. Forgive me. Why, God, why didn't they call me before they left for the city?"

His car kept running until it was out of gas.

What Constant confided to God, no one in the village ever knew. And a garrulous arrow of wild ducks shot towards the south.